"I called you an idiot."

"We're childhood friends, actually."

Yuki Suou

A proper young lady from a family of former nobility. She is the student council's publicist and Masachika's childhood friend. She is also known as the noble princess, one of the two so-called "beautiful princesses" of Seiren Academy alongside Alisa.

Alisa Mikhailovna Kujou

A model student at the top of her class and currently the accountant for the student council. She is also known as the solitary princess, one of the two "beautiful princesses" of Seiren Academy. While she often scolds Masachika about his behavior, sometimes…

"What were these bashful sweet nothings Alisa always whispered in Russian?"

Masachika Kuze

An unmotivated underachiever who routinely stays up late indulging in his nerdy hobbies. The girl who sits next to him in class, Alisa, constantly gets after him. While his grades may be on the lower end, he actually understands Russian.

Contents

Alya
Sometimes Hides Her
Feelings in
Russian

1

Sunsunsun
Illustration by Momoco

New York

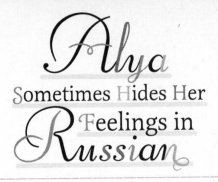

Alya Sometimes Hides Her Feelings in Russian

1 Sunsunsun

Translation by Matthew Rutsohn
Cover art by Momoco

This book is a work of fiction. Names, characters, places, and incidents are the product of the author's imagination or are used fictitiously. Any resemblance to actual events, locales, or persons, living or dead, is coincidental.

TOKIDOKI BOSOTTO ROSHIAGO DE DERERU TONARI NO ARYA SAN Vol.1
©Sunsunsun, Momoco 2021
First published in Japan in 2021 by KADOKAWA CORPORATION, Tokyo.
English translation rights arranged with KADOKAWA CORPORATION, Tokyo, through TUTTLE-MORI AGENCY, INC., Tokyo.

English translation © 2022 by Yen Press, LLC.

Yen On
150 West 30th Street, 19th Floor
New York, NY 10001

Visit us at yenpress.com • facebook.com/yenpress • twitter.com/yenpress • yenpress.tumblr.com
instagram.com/yenpress

First Yen On Edition: October 2022
Edited by Yen On Editorial: Leilah Labossiere, Rachel Mimms
Designed by Yen Press Design: Liz Parlett

Yen On is an imprint of Yen Press, LLC.
The Yen On name and logo are trademarks of Yen Press, LLC.

The publisher is not responsible for websites (or their content) that are not owned by the publisher.

Library of Congress Cataloging-in-Publication Data
Names: Sunsunsun, author. | Momoco, illustrator. | Rutsohn, Matt, translator.
Title: Alya sometimes hides her feelings in Russian / Sunsunsun ; illustration by Momoco ; translation by Matthew Rutsohn.
Other titles: Tokidoki bosotto roshiago de dereru tonari no Arya san. English
Description: First Yen On edition. | New York, NY : Yen On, 2022-
Identifiers: LCCN 2022029973 | ISBN 9781975347840 (v. 1 ; trade paperback)
Subjects: CYAC: Language and languages—Fiction. | Friendship—Fiction. | Schools—Fiction. | LCGFT: Humorous fiction. | School fiction. | Light novels.
Classification: LCC PZ7.1.S8676 Ar 2022 | DDC [Fic]—dc23
LC record available at https://lccn.loc.gov/2022029973

ISBNs: 978-1-9753-4784-0 (paperback)
        978-1-9753-4785-7 (ebook)

10 9 8 7 6 5 4 3 2 1

LSC-C

Printed in the United States of America

The Solitary Princess and Her Lazy Neighbor

Seiren Private Academy was an integrated middle school, high school, and university, and over the years, this top-level institution had produced countless graduates who went on to work in the world of politics and business. In the prestigious school's long, rich history, it had even been said that the majority of students were from noble and elite families.

Students walked in droves down the tree-lined path toward the distinguished schoolhouse. Friends and classmates chatted cheerfully on their way to the building, but when a certain female student walked through the school gate, everything changed. Every student who saw her followed her with their gaze, their eyes wide in surprise and wonder.

"Whoa. Who's that? She's stunning!"

"How do you not remember her? She repped the new students at the entrance ceremony the other day and gave a speech. That's *Maria's* little sister."

"I was way in the back at the ceremony, so I could barely see anything. *Sigh*... She looks like an angel..."

"She really does. I'm a girl and older than her, but she still makes me weak at the knees."

Unlike most Japanese people, she had milky-white skin that was so pale, it was almost translucent, and her almond-shaped eyes were like glittering sapphires. Her long, silver hair was pulled back into a half ponytail that twinkled in the morning sun. The distinct facial features she inherited from her Russian father were softened by the beauty she got from her Japanese mother. In addition to her unique features, she was tall for a girl, with long limbs and an hourglass figure. She had a body that women around the world could only dream of having.

Her name was Alisa Mikhailovna Kujou. After transferring to Seiren Private Academy last year as a third-year middle school student, she worked her way up to claim the top spot in her class. She was excellent at sports and would be the student council accountant starting this year, to boot. With all that talent, it was hard to not see her as a flawless superwoman.

"Hey, look."

"Huh? Oh, it's Kujou! Must be my lucky morning."

"Dude, go say hello to her."

"No way! I'm not worthy!"

"That's not like you at all. You hit on cute girls all the time, no matter who they are. You telling me you're too scared to even say hello?"

"Are you insane?! She's way out of my league! She's out of my universe, in fact! You go talk to her if you want to so badly!"

"And risk getting killed by the other guys because I said something stupid? Not happening."

Boys and girls alike watched her enviously, naturally slowing their pace and moving out of her way while she confidently walked by without a care in the world. That was when one male student approached her, and a clamor arose from the surrounding students.

"Hey. Nice weather we're having this morning, huh?"

Without even stopping, Alisa glanced at the cheerfully smiling male student, noticed he was an upperclassman by the color of his tie, and gave a small bow.

"Good morning."

"Yeah, good morning. Nice to meet you, too, since I think this is the first time we've ever talked. I'm Andou. I'm in the same class as your sister."

"Is that so?"

The teen named Andou had dyed brown hair and wore a slightly worn-out school uniform with silver chains peeking out from under his collar. He was a good-looking guy and followed the latest fashion trends, but Alisa seemed indifferent. Unlike the surrounding girls squealing over his sweet smile, Alisa didn't even bat an eye.

"Your sister's told me a lot about you…so I've been wanting to meet you. Maybe we could have lunch together today? Whaddaya say?"

"No, thank you," she replied without a hint of hesitation.

Andou smiled weakly. "Ha-ha… Harsh… Then do you think we could at least exchange numbers? I want to get to know you better."

"Sorry, but I couldn't be any less interested. Now, if you'll excuse me. Oh, and one more thing…"

Alisa then swiftly turned her gaze back to Andou and lifted her hand toward his neck. His smile faded at the sight of her cold stare and delicate fingers, and eyes wide, he began to retreat.

"…That's against school rules," Alisa snapped coldly as she pointed at the silver chain around his neck, unfazed by his flustered behavior.

"Bye."

She left him with that single word before walking away. The area instantly exploded with gossip and chatter as the students who had been watching with bated breath suddenly began to speak up.

"Whoa… She just kicked Andou to the curb. *Andou*, a high schooler. He's, like, the most popular guy in his grade, too. She truly is the solitary princess…"

"Her standards must be stupidly high. If he wasn't good enough, then who is?"

"Maybe she doesn't even like guys? That'd really suck, though. She's so hot."

"Or maybe it's a good thing? You know, since no one's ever gonna steal her away."

"Good point. She'd be closer to an actual idol like that, and I could just continue to admire her without ever having to worry about another guy getting in the way. Hell, might as well just worship her at this point."

"Dude, now you're just being creepy... I know what you mean, though."

Alisa stepped into the school building, completely unaware of what her classmates were saying about her. At her shoe locker, she changed into her slippers, then headed for her classroom. She had already forgotten about the guy she gave the cold shoulder to a few moments ago. After all, an unremarkable event like that wasn't even worth remembering to Alisa. Being the center of attention and getting hit on were daily occurrences for her.

When she arrived at her classroom, she opened the door and was met with the gazes of her classmates. This was a daily occurrence as well, so Alisa simply headed over to her seat by the window in the very last row, unconcerned by the attention. After placing her bag by her desk, she casually glanced at the seat to her right, which was assigned to a male student merely due to the alphabetical seating order. For more than a year already, this first-year high school student, Masachika Kuze, had held this coveted position next to one of the two "beautiful princesses" in their grade. Most male students would kill to be able to sit next to her.

"..."

He was lying on his desk, sound asleep before class had even started. Alisa, whose expression had remained unchanged, glared at such an unbecoming sight for a student at so prestigious a school.

"Good morning, Kuze."

"..."

Masachika, who was using his arms as a pillow over his desk, didn't respond to her greeting. He was completely out cold. Alisa, after essentially being ignored, glared harder.

"M-Masachika, bro. Wake up," discreetly whispered the classmate who sat diagonally to their right, eyes twitching nervously as he watched the events unfold. But before Masachika even had time to open his eyes...

Whack!

"Gfffeee?!"

...all of a sudden, Masachika's desk slid sideways with a *bang*, causing him to throw his head up with a squeal. Alisa had just kicked the side of his desk. The spectating students could not help but sigh in unison. It was already common knowledge in their grade that Alisa, despite being a high-achieving, well-behaved model student, was indifferent toward others and kept to herself. Yet she was exceptionally strict toward Masachika, who was the epitome of a slacker.

Since it was practically an everyday occurrence, everyone was used to seeing Alisa harshly criticize Masachika while he basically brushed off whatever she said.

"Good morning, Kuze. Did you stay up all night watching anime again?"

Alisa greeted her seemingly confused classmate once more while wearing an innocent expression. After blinking a few times and looking up, Masachika shrugged as if he could guess what had happened.

"Oh... Hey, Alya. And yeah, that's the gist of it."

"Alya" was Alisa's Russian nickname, a pet name of endearment, and while plenty of people called her that when she wasn't around, Masachika was the only guy in school who would call her Alya to her face. Whether Masachika was being thoughtless or Alisa was simply being tolerant was still a mystery, though. Either way, despite Alisa's extremely cold gaze and the fact that she had just kicked his desk to wake him up, Masachika didn't seem intimidated. His classmates' gazes expressed both annoyance and admiration, but Masachika wasn't trying to do anything special...because he had no idea what he was doing.

"*Gfffeee*"? *Who screams like that? Pfft! I've never heard a weirder scream in my life.*

There was no disgust in Alisa's eyes as she looked down at him. If anything, it looked as if there was a smile hidden in them. It was obvious she secretly enjoyed making him squeal and jump out of his seat.

"You never learn, do you? You need to cut back on the anime if it's going to make you fall asleep in class," she nagged and took a seat next to him, as if Masachika couldn't tell how much she was enjoying this.

"Actually, the anime ended at one in the morning. It was the discussion afterward that took so long."

"'Discussion'? Oh, you mean when people go online to share how they felt about the episode?"

"Hmm? No. I called my friend, and we ended up talking on the phone for the next two hours about the episode."

"You're an idiot."

Masachika stared into the distance and smiled while basking in Alisa's reproachful gaze.

"I'm an idiot, huh? Yeah... Discussing something you love, regardless of the time or place—if that makes me an idiot, then so be it..."

"I'm sorry. You're not an idiot. You're a hopeless, brain-dead moron."

"You seem to be in a good mood today, too, Alya."

He jokingly shrugged off Alisa's brutal comments. She shook her head as if to say, "There's no way to deal with him," when all of a sudden, the bell rang, alerting the students that class was going to start in three minutes. As the other students returned to their seats, Alisa faced forward, taking her notebook, textbooks, and other school supplies out of her bag. In the room of well-behaved students, which one would simply expect at such a prestigious school, only Masachika stretched out his arms wide. He let out a big yawn as tears welled in his eyes. Alisa, who had her eyes on him the entire time, suddenly turned her gaze toward the window, cracked a smile, and whispered in Russian:

^{Cutie}
"Милашка..."

"*Yaaawn*. You say something?" asked Masachika, having caught her whisper with his keen hearing.

"I said what you were doing was unseemly. That's all," she replied, feigning ignorance.

"My apologies, then," he replied, acting as though she must have been referring to his yawning, so he covered his mouth when he next yawned. Alisa scornfully raised an eyebrow at him, then quickly faced the window once more and smiled. Keeping her expression hidden to Masachika, she gleefully cheered in her head:

You're such a dummy! You really have no idea! Hee-hee!

She covered her smile by pretending to rest her elbow on the desk, but Masachika stared at her back with some pity.

Too bad I understood what you really said.

Alisa had no idea.

She had no idea that Masachika understood Russian.

And she didn't know that he could understand every sweet word she whispered about him.

Never would the other students realize the humorous, slightly embarrassing conversations they were actually having behind what seemed like bickering.

CHAPTER 1

Who wouldn't be frustrated if they missed the free daily character summon?

"Hmm?"

After rummaging through his desk, peeking into his backpack, and checking his locker in the back of the classroom, Masachika started to panic slightly. He couldn't find his textbook for the next class, and when he looked up at the clock, he realized he had less than two minutes before it started. He could sprint to the classroom next door and ask his sister to borrow her book, but he decided not to bother her. He had no choice but to lean to his left, clasp his hands together in supplication, and whisper, "Alya, sorry, but do you think we could share your chemistry book?"

"You forgot your book again?" replied Alya, rolling her eyes irritably.

"Yeah, I probably left it at home."

"Fine." She sighed.

"Thanks!"

Masachika hastily scooted his desk next to hers.

"How do you forget your book so often? You don't seem to have changed one bit even after starting high school."

"Hey, can you blame me? We have way too many textbooks."

Seiren Academy had an absurd number of textbooks required for their classes due to being a college-preparatory private school. Therefore, each subject demanded numerous textbooks and reference books, and some classes even had supplementary books created by the teachers themselves. And yet their schoolbags hadn't been upgraded once in the past few decades. Whether the school was simply being respectful of tradition was unclear, but what *was* clear was that one day's worth of textbooks was enough to fill their bags until they were on the verge of tearing at the seams. Therefore, most students left all their textbooks at school. This seemed a bit tricky for Masachika to manage, however.

"It wasn't in my desk when I checked yesterday, so I thought it was in my locker, but…it looks like I was wrong."

"You should have checked your locker to make sure, then. This only happens because you don't double-check which books you take home and which ones you leave here."

"Well, you got me there."

"I'm not in the mood for sarcasm."

"Oof. Harsh."

Alisa shrugged and rolled her eyes at Masachika's apathetic demeanor and monotone voice. She then pulled all her chemistry textbooks out of her desk and turned to Masachika with a questioning gaze.

"So? Which textbook did you need?"

"Oh, that one. The blue one."

After opening the blue reference book, she placed it in the middle of their desks. Masachika promptly thanked her and prepared for the teacher's lecture…when the sandman suddenly came out of nowhere and attacked.

Oh god. I'm feeling sleepy.

Having PE second period didn't help the fact that he was sleep-deprived. Although he resisted the sandman while the teacher was writing on the board, sleep instantly gained the upper hand when the teacher began asking the students questions. Their back-and-forth started to sound like a lullaby of sorts, causing Masachika to slowly doze off…

"Nnng?!"

Immediately, the tip of a mechanical pencil was jammed into his side.

I-it went…right between my ribs!

Masachika silently groaned in agony and shot a reproachful look toward the girl beside him...who instantly returned his gaze with a contemptuous stare, causing him to flinch. Her narrowed blue eyes were eloquently saying, "Wow. Pretty bold of you to sleep after begging me to share my textbook with you."

"Sorry."

Masachika whispered an apology while facing straight ahead, now wide awake and alert.

"Hmph."

But the only response he got was a snort of contempt.

"All right, then. Anyone want to guess what goes into the blank here? Hmm... How about you, Kuze?"

"Huh? Oh, okay."

Masachika stood up in a fluster after being called on by the teacher without warning. Of course, there was no way he would know the answer, since he'd been dozing off up until a few seconds ago. In fact, he didn't even know what problem the teacher was talking about. He looked to his side for help, but Alisa didn't even glance in his direction, pretending not to notice.

"What's wrong? We don't have all day."

"Uh... Um..."

Right as he was about to consider admitting he didn't know the answer, Alisa suddenly sighed while tapping on a certain line in the textbook.

"...! The answer is number two! Copper!"

Masachika internally thanked Alisa and responded to the teacher with the answer being presented to him, but...

"Wrong."

"Huh?" Masachika grunted with embarrassment after immediately being shot down.

The hell?! It wasn't number two!

Masachika screamed internally, swiftly looking over to his side, but Alisa was still pretending like she didn't notice him... However, after a closer look, he noticed she was faintly smirking.

"How about you, Kujou? Do you know the answer?"

"Yes, it's number eight: nickel."

"Yep. Good job. Kuze, stop daydreaming and start paying attention. Got it?"

"Y-yes, sir..."

Masachika sat down dejectedly but immediately started whispering complaints to Alisa.

"Why'd you tell me the wrong answer?"

"I was just showing you where the answers were."

"You liar! You were clearly pointing at number two!"

"That's quite the accusation."

"You're laughing at me! I can see it in your eyes!"

Masachika was on the verge of screaming out loud. Alisa smirked contemptuously and snorted with laughter. She then whispered in Russian:

"<Cutie.>"

It took everything Masachika had to keep his cheek from twitching, to the point that his hands were almost trembling, but he eventually managed to keep his composure and acted like he didn't understand her affectionate remark.

"What was that?" he asked her, keeping his voice low.

"I called you an idiot."

You liarrrrrr!!

He was shouting in his head, but he made sure to keep a straight face.

Masachika could understand Russian because his grandfather on his father's side loved Russia. It all started in elementary school when he temporarily lived with his grandfather, who made him watch countless Russian movies. Masachika himself had never been to Russia, nor did he have any Russian relatives. He never spoke about it at school, either, so the only person who knew he understood Russian was his younger sister, who was in the class next door. Furthermore, he told his sister not to tell a soul, so there was no way anyone else would ever find out. In hindsight, Masachika wished he had told Alisa sooner, but it was far too late now. This form of humiliation play, where the beautiful girl next to him only spoke affectionately of him in Russian, was all his fault, so he had no choice but to take the hit on the chin.

Masachika's cheeks turned red, his lips pressing together tightly as he desperately struggled to hide the indescribable embarrassment welling in his chest. Alisa, however, thought he was trying to control his anger and amusingly whispered, "<He looks like a baby.>"

Masachika suddenly imagined himself as a baby with Alisa poking his cheeks, a big grin on her face.

It's war she wants, huh?

Once he realized she was being condescending and toying with him, his expression instantly turned serious.

Who are you callin' a baby? I hope you're ready for this, you punk.

Masachika glanced up at the clock to check how much time was left before class ended.

Eleven forty. Looks like I've got ten minutes to get back at her—

Suddenly, his eyes opened wide as he had a shocking realization.

Oh, crap! I still haven't gotten my game's free daily character summon!

Masachika had made a critical mistake. He usually made sure to check before he left the house or on the way to homeroom, but he'd been so sleepy that morning that he hadn't been thinking straight.

That was a close one. Good job remembering, me. It looks like I'm gonna be busy during break.

His thoughts had completely shifted into nerd mode, and he completely stopped caring about how Alisa had treated him like a baby. It was probably inevitable for someone so simpleminded to be called a baby, but Masachika was oblivious to this fact. He idly sat and behaved until class ended…but the moment the teacher walked out the door, he hurriedly moved his desk back to its original position, whipped out his phone, and immediately booted up an app.

"Using smartphones on campus is against school rules unless it's for an emergency or for studying. Pretty bold of you to be doing that

in front of me, a student council officer," scolded Alisa, her brow knit
in disapproval.

"Then this isn't against school rules. It's an emergency."

"...Okay, fine. I'll bite. What's the emergency?"

She stared at him reproachfully, expecting his answer to be something absurd.

"The free character drop ends in ten minutes," Masachika replied
with unwarranted confidence.

"Do you want your phone confiscated?"

"I trust you, homie. ☆ You wouldn't do that to me." Masachika
awkwardly winked and gave her a thumbs-up, but Alisa's reproachful gaze only grew sterner.

"Wanna bet?"

"Oh man. I hope it's a rare drop... Now that I think about it, that
was the first time I actually winked in forever. It's a lot harder than it
looks, huh?" Masachika was rambling with his eyes locked on the
phone in his hands as if Alisa's words had gone in one ear and out
the other.

"What are you blabbering about?"

"You know, winking. You see idol groups do it sometimes, but
there aren't even that many celebrities who can actually pull it off."

"You really think so?"

"Huh? You don't think it's hard? Your cheeks and the corners of
your lips don't awkwardly rise when you wink?"

"No."

"Oh, really? Then let's see it. Show me a good wink."

He lifted his head and curled his lips into a provocative smirk.
One of Alisa's eyebrows suddenly twitched over her glum expression,
and the nearby students who were eavesdropping began whispering.
Alisa immediately felt their gazes on her while she turned to face
Masachika with incredulity, and she sighed deeply.

"*Sigh...* Like this?"

She then tilted her head and shot him a superb wink. No

unnecessary muscle in her face moved as she perfectly and naturally batted her eye.

"Whoaaa!"

The classmates who were fortunate enough to catch a glimpse of the solitary princess's once-in-a-lifetime wink exhibition squealed while sparsely clapping with admiration and astonishment. And yet Masachika, the guy who had asked her to wink in the first place…

"The SSR Tsukuyomi?! Yesss!! …Oh, sorry. I wasn't paying attention."

"Say good-bye to your phone."

"Noooooo!" screamed Masachika as Alisa mercilessly yanked his phone out of his hand.

She stood there with a hand on her hip and looked down at him. It wasn't clear if the faint tinge of red in her cheeks was because she was blushing or infuriated. It incidentally almost looked as if Masachika was getting back at her for what she did to him during class, but that wasn't even on his mind. Some could argue that his lack of malice made what he did all the more wicked, though.

"H-hey, did you get a good picture of that?"

Alisa instantly noticed the three male classmates who were muttering with their heads together.

"I tried, but I couldn't from this angle."

"Heh, I got you, fam. Snagged a pic the moment she winked."

"Whoa! Seriously?! You're a freaking god!"

"You better send me a copy! I'll give you a thousand yen!"

"Say good-bye to your phones."

""""Ack?! Kujou?!"""" the three boys shrieked in unison as the phones with Alisa's nonconsensual photograph were confiscated.

"Why are you taking our phones?! We weren't—!"

"You weren't what?"

"Oh, uh… Nothing… Never mind…"

The once-tenacious male student promptly cowered under her sharp glare. And who could blame him? Even the toughest of men would probably flinch if Alisa looked down at them with her eyes wide and her jaw firmly set. It was equivalent to facing a furious blizzard on the tundra. Their classmates, who had also been excited to see Alisa wink, suddenly and swiftly averted their gazes and held their breaths, hoping to go unnoticed and wait out the storm. Alisa slowly returned to her desk with four smartphones in hand as if she were walking through a desolate field of snow. Her classmates simply hung their heads and waited for her to pass—and yet there was still one student who wasn't intimidated in the least by her imposing appearance.

"Please forgive meee. I beg you, have mercyyy."

Masachika threw himself before Alisa's feet with his hands together as he pitifully begged for his phone back. The fact that he was still joking around was the reason why everyone stared at him like he was a hero (or an idiot).

"Come on, give me a break. Who wouldn't be excited to get an SSR character during the free daily summon? I couldn't *not* look."

It didn't help that he was trying to justify his actions, either. His peers raised their eyebrows as if they couldn't believe what they were seeing. Her expression still contemptuous, Alisa looked down at Masachika's confiscated smartphone.

"...The SSR version of Tsukuyomi? Isn't Tsukuyomi a god from Japanese mythology? Why does she have silver hair instead of black?"

"Huh? Oh... Beats me. Probably wanted her to look moon-ish, since she's the moon goddess. Anyway, it doesn't matter. She's cute, and that's all that matters."

"...Hmm."

Masachika had a shit-eating grin on his face, causing Alisa to narrow her eyes. The temperature plummeted until it was as cold as the North Pole.

"Huh? What the...?" he mumbled as his smile grew tense.

"...Anyway, I'm going to be holding on to this until school's over. I'm turning it off as well."

"Wait! I haven't saved yet! It might not autosave if you just shut it off!"

He legitimately panicked as Alisa mercilessly hovered her finger over the power button.

"It's me you've got a problem with! Tsukuyomi had nothing to do with this! I don't care what happens to me, but please don't hurt her!"

"Why are you acting like I'm the bad guy here?"

Masachika made it sound like the love of his life had been taken hostage, so Alisa couldn't help but simultaneously look down at *and* on him. She then sighed and shoved his smartphone back into his hands.

"Thank you, kind madam. Thank you."

"…Hmph." Alisa, now in a foul mood, snorted unapologetically and scrutinized Masachika as he remained prostrate with his phone between both hands. She ended up returning the other three smartphones to their owners as well. The storm seemed to have passed; she made sure they deleted the photo of her, and she returned to her desk, plopping back down in her seat.

"Man, it really is Tsukuyomi. I still can't believe I got her…"

"…"

Alisa twirled her hair with her finger and glanced at Masachika, who stared at his smartphone with sparkles in his eyes. She pouted.

"<My hair's silver, too…>"

Jealousy from out of left field. Masachika froze.

"…What was that?"

He lifted his head, his expression tense, as if he couldn't simply let that comment slip by. Alisa stopped twirling her hair.

"I just called you a degenerate gamer, that's all," she hissed in disgust, shooting him a chilling glare.

"Hey, come on. That was rude."

"H-hmph."

Alisa recoiled at Masachika's unusually sharp tone and severe expression, but she almost immediately added:

"I didn't say anything that's not true."

She sternly glared back at him, and the mounting pressure piqued their classmates' attention once more.

"You're calling me a degenerate even though I play this game for free? Don't you think that's rude to real addicts who blow through their life savings on these games?" protested Masachika with a completely serious expression.

"You're right. I'm sure they feel insulted to be lumped into the same group as you."

"Ouch?!"

Alisa glared at Masachika's obscenely smug expression as if she were looking at garbage, and he clutched his chest in pain as though her gaze physically hurt him. After his theatrical performance, Alisa sighed deeply like she couldn't put up with him anymore.

"Ugh... And here I thought you were being serious for a change."

"Hey, now. I'm offended. I'm *always* serious. You could even say that being serious is one of my strengths."

"That has to be the biggest lie of the century."

"We're only, like, a quarter of the way into the century, though!"

"*Sigh...* Just put your phone away."

After shrugging, she rested her chin on her hand. She looked exhausted.

"Yeah, I probably went a little too far." Masachika shrugged, too, after he saw the look on her face. But right as he was about to put his phone away, his ears were greeted again with Russian, and he stiffened.

"<He would be so cool if he was more serious.>"

A tingle went up his spine, and he instinctively turned to his side.

"What was that?"

"I said, 'I shouldn't have expected anything from you.'"

"Uh-huh..."

"Yep."

Masachika inwardly screamed, *You liarrrrrr!* Alisa also inwardly stuck out her tongue at him, and his cheek twitched because he knew exactly what she was thinking.

Ahhh!! I...understand...everything...you're...thinking...and... saying...!!

He wondered how good it would feel to scream that, but it would only hurt him in the long run if he did.

Grrr...

It was still frustrating, despite knowing he couldn't say anything. He ground his teeth as he thought about how he was going to outwit this tsundere in disguise...when all of a sudden, the classroom door opened.

"Okay, guys. I know I'm early, but I've got a big lesson planned for the day, so let's get started... Wait. Kuze, why do you have your phone out?"

Only when the teacher pointed it out did Masachika notice he was still holding his smartphone.

"Oh, uh... I was just looking up something for one of our assignments..."

"Kujou, is he telling the truth?"

"No. He was playing a game on his phone."

"Hey?!"

"Figured. Get over here, Kuze! I'm taking your phone!"

"You *figured*?! What's that supposed to mean?!"

Alisa let out a sigh as she watched Masachika plead with their teacher every step of the way.

"*Haaah...* What an idiot," she muttered with clear disgust. Never would her classmates know that her lips were actually curled into a faint smile...

"Whoa?! Is Princess Alya smiling?!"

"Whoaaa! Now's our chance!"

"Work, dammit! Work! Why isn't my camera app working?!"

"Teacher, these three are playing with their smartphones, too."

""Nooo!!"""

...with the exception of those three idiots.

CHAPTER 2

I have friends, you know?

The cafeteria was echoing with chatter and rustling as students passed by one another with trays in their hands. Masachika had come here with his friends for lunch, and they were in the middle of staring at the menu at the entrance while they pondered what they would order.

"Oh, hey. Look. They've got something new."

One item with the word *new* underneath it had caught Masachika's attention: mapo-tofu ramen, a simple dish of spicy mapo tofu dumped on top of ramen—and a godsend for someone like Masachika, who loved ramen and spicy food.

"Mapo-tofu ramen? So it's Chinese food topped with Chinese food." Takeshi Maruyama laughed; he had been friends with Masachika ever since middle school. Takeshi had a shaved head and was slightly shorter than Masachika.

"Takeshi, ramen technically isn't Chinese food, though."

"Wait. It isn't?"

"Nope. The word *ramen* itself is actually Japanese."

Hikaru Kiyomiya was the one who shared that piece of trivia. He had also been friends with Masachika ever since middle school. He was a delicate, beautiful, androgynous young man with naturally light hair and eyes. He was one of the most gorgeous guys in the entire school, which was evident by the fact that every girl walking into the cafeteria gushed over him as they passed by.

"Have you two already decided what you're going to get?"

"Yep."

"Yes."

After exchanging brief nods, they walked into the cafeteria, then placed a handkerchief and some tissues on a table to claim their seats before heading over to the line for food. Once they put in their orders, they returned to their seats and began eating. Of course, it was Masachika's mapo-tofu ramen that became the focus of attention.

"Whoa... It's even redder than it was in the picture."

"That looks way too spicy."

"Not at all. It needs to be spicier if anything. Still tastes good, though."

Sitting across from Masachika, Takeshi and Hikaru watched in obvious disbelief as he slurped up his noodles, but Masachika himself was calm as could be.

"Hmm... Let me try some of your noodles."

"Ooh, me too."

"Sure."

"Thanks... What the...?! This is spicy as hell!"

"Ack! It burns going down...!"

They dug into the ramen with their chopsticks, but the instant they took a bite, they frowned and reached for their cups.

"Okay, guys. You can't call something spicy if the steam doesn't make your eyes water," Masachika chided.

"That is a bizarre definition of spicy."

"You can say that again."

"Real spicy ramen burns your lips to the point where you can't even slurp them up like ordinary noodles."

"'Spicy'? Sounds more like *feisty*. Am I right?"

"I can't even imagine ramen that spicy."

"It would tear through your stomach, too, of course."

"The hell, man? Don't eat stuff that you know's going to give you diarrhea," Takeshi replied promptly, when all of a sudden, there was commotion at the cafeteria's entrance. They instinctively looked toward the noise and saw three girls walk in.

"Oh, it's the student council... I don't see the president or the vice president anywhere, though. Still not every day you see three of them together like this. It's… Wow."

Takeshi gasped as he watched them walk by, his peers *ooh*ing and *aah*ing the whole time. The guys were drooling over them while the girls looked up to them like idols.

"The Kujou sisters are so beautiful, aren't they?" Hikaru muttered softly as he looked at Alisa, who stood out the most due to her silver hair, and the slightly shorter girl walking in front of her. This girl, Maria Mikhailovna Kujou, was a second-year student and the student council secretary. She was Alisa's older sister by one year and was called Masha by those close to her. However, neither her hair color nor style were anything like her sister's. While Maria had fair skin, it was more like *light compared with the average Japanese person's*, unlike Alisa's almost translucent milky-white skin. Her shoulder-length wavy hair was light brown, and she had bright, chocolate-colored, gentle almond-shaped eyes. Her figure, including her baby face, was also closer to that of the average Japanese person. It was almost hard to tell which one of them was older at first glance when she stood next to Alisa, who had a slim, tall, and mature figure. However, one glance below Maria's face would clear up any misunderstanding. She had the body of an older sister. More specifically, she had huge breasts. And a huge rear as well. While Alisa had a figure that stood out from the average Japanese person's, Maria had an even more "feminine" body. Her voluptuous figure and inherently gentle personality and style gave her a very maternal appearance, which was unexpected from some-one her age. In fact, she was even called Madonna by some of her peers.

"Maria is so cute. I'd love to get to know her."

"I heard she has a boyfriend, though," chimed in Hikaru.

"Yeah, I know! Dammit! Who's the lucky guy?!"

Takeshi's dreamy expression instantly turned into a teeth-grinding scowl, causing Masachika to raise an eyebrow in surprise.

"Wait. Takeshi? 'Who's the lucky guy'? I thought you of all people would know."

"Not sure what you mean by 'you of all people,' but whatever. All I know is it's some Russian guy."

"Huh."

"I wonder if it's a long-distance relationship. I heard that Maria goes to Russia quite a bit."

Hikaru had a point. The Kujou sisters often went back and forth between Russia and Japan due to their father's work. Alisa had even lived in Russia until she was five, before coming to Japan for her first year of elementary school. She then went back to Russia during her fourth year and returned to Japan during her third year of middle school.

"I guess if they're long-distance, that means they've been dating for over a year now... I don't stand a chance."

"True... Besides, she's apparently turned down every guy who has asked her out so far because of this boyfriend."

"Takeshi wouldn't stand a chance, in any case," chimed in Masachika, forcing his friend to confront this cold, harsh fact.

"Oh, shut up! Don't act all cocky just 'cause you and Princess Alya are close!" Takeshi furiously snorted.

"Yeah, I don't know about that. It's more like she puts up with me."

"Still better than her being completely uninterested in you. She barely talks to anyone, and if you try to approach her, she basically just cuts you off with some businesslike reply."

"Well, we have been sitting next to each other for over a year now..."

"Even then, man. I mean, I'm pretty sure you're the only person who can get away with calling her by her nickname to her face."

"Yeah, I guess..."

"Man... I wish the solitary princess would let me call her by her nickname, too..."

"Why don't you try, then? Be aggressive. She's your classmate, too, you know?" suggested Masachika. Takeshi grimaced as he waved his hand in front of his face.

"No way, man. I wouldn't even know how to approach someone that perfect."

"Doesn't mean you should be sneaking photos of her."

"Can you blame me? Look how beautiful she is," argued Takeshi with an air of innocence before Masachika's reproachful gaze. If it wasn't obvious already, Takeshi was one of the three guys who'd had his smartphone confiscated that morning for secretly taking pictures of Alisa. In fact, he was the ringleader of the group.

"*Sigh...* I could stare at her all day. She is legit eyegasm material. And her sister? Put those two together, and I'm gonna need an extra pair of underwear."

"Takeshi, that was seriously gross."

"Yeah, I legit threw up a little in my mouth."

Even Takeshi's two friends were disgusted by his euphoric expression as he gawked at the Kujou sisters, but Takeshi himself looked back at Masachika and Hikaru as if they were the ones with the problem.

"What? Don't tell me you guys disagree. I've never seen anyone as pretty as them in my life."

"I mean, I admit they're good-looking, but you shouldn't worship them. Alya's actually kind of funny once you get to know her...in more ways than one."

"'Ooh, look at me. I'm Masachika. I know the *real* Alya.' Humblebrag much?"

"I wasn't bragging."

"So she's 'kind of funny,' huh? I'm impressed you of all people can say something like that with a straight face."

"Do I detect a hint of sarcasm, Hikaru? Trying to tell me to know my place?"

"That's not what I meant. I was just saying how I admire that you could say something like that about someone who gets after you every single day."

"Oh..."

Masachika looked away and gave a slight nod. One of the reasons he was fine with Alisa scolding him every day was because she was right. But even more than that, it was because what she whispered to herself in Russian occasionally was always extremely sweet. Plus, Alisa wouldn't be scolding him all the time if she actually hated him to begin with. She would just ignore him…which meant that deep down inside, she probably enjoyed their exchanges. That was why Masachika didn't let her complaints bother him. He would never be able to tell anyone that, though.

"Anyway, how about trying to talk to her? Nothing big. You might be surprised to find you two have a lot in common."

"Yeah… But after what happened last year? I don't know."

Masachika nodded back at Takeshi with understanding. A young, beautiful transfer student had suddenly appeared last year like a comet. She, Alisa, instantly became the center of attention. Transfer students in general were extremely rare at Seiren Academy. The reason for this was simple: The entrance exam for transfer students was extremely difficult. Although the highly selective school was tough to get into already, the exam for transfer students was so hard that only a tenth of the current students, at most, could pass it. Nevertheless, not only did Alisa pass the entrance exam for transfer students, but she also got the highest scores on her midterms in her grade. Plus, she was beautiful. It would be more surprising if she wasn't the center of attention. But while countless guys and girls tried to befriend her, she always kept her distance and never tried to get close to anyone. In no time flat, people started calling her the solitary princess.

"If I'm going to try to make a move on one of them, it's going to be Yuki. By process of elimination, of course," claimed Takeshi while looking at one of the girls lined up to order food. She had long, black, shiny hair that went down to her waist, and while she was small in stature, she had a well-proportioned feminine body. It didn't appear to be as sensual as Alisa's or Maria's at first glance. However, despite her dainty looks, she displayed elegance through her firm posture and graceful gestures as if to hint at a proper noble upbringing.

She, Yuki Suou, was a first-year student and the student council publicist. She was the eldest daughter from a family of former nobility who had worked as diplomats for generations. She was genuinely one of the elites. Just like how students called Alisa the solitary princess, Yuki's peers referred to her as the noble princess due to her high social skills and refined behavior, making her the other "beautiful princess" on campus.

"Like, I know she's out of my league, but she's easy to talk to, so at least I still have a chance, unlike with Princess Alya."

As Takeshi continuously nodded to himself, Hikaru skeptically tilted his head.

"Do you really have a chance, though? Yuki is known for having turned down more guys than even Alisa."

"Mmm… Yeah… Maybe she's not looking for a boyfriend? Or maybe she has a fiancé already, just like real nobility? So, Masachika? What's the deal with her?"

"Why are you asking me?"

"Who else would I ask? You two *grew up together*," argued Takeshi, emphasizing each word as his eyes smoldered with jealousy. Masachika sighed.

"She doesn't have a fiancé as far as I know. I don't know if she's interested in dating, though."

"Then go ask her."

"No."

"Why?! Come on! Be a friend!"

"Real friends don't use their friendship to pressure others into doing something."

"Oh. Yes, I agree with Masachika on that."

"Ack!"

Takeshi was immediately silenced by the verbal cross fire hitting him from every direction. When Masachika just happened to glance over at the food line, he saw that the three girls had begun looking for empty seats with their trays in hand. It looked like there was nowhere left to sit until all of a sudden, a student in the corner of the cafeteria waved someone over. After Maria said something to the other two, she began walking over to the girl waving, most likely her friend or classmate. The other two kept looking around the cafeteria until Yuki's and Masachika's eyes met. She recognized him right away and her gaze slid to his side where there were two empty seats at the end of the table.

Guess I know where they're sitting now.

Right as Masachika's gut told him that, Yuki said something to Alisa and started walking straight toward them, which flustered Takeshi and made him immediately straighten his posture.

"Masachika, are these seats taken?"

All eyes were on Yuki, so the sharp crease that appeared in Alisa's brow the moment those words left Yuki's lips went unnoticed.

"Oh, uh. No, they're all yours. You guys don't mind, right?"

"O-of course not."

"Be my guest."

"Thanks," she replied with a gorgeous smile before walking around to the other side of the table and sitting next to Masachika. Alisa then sat next to Takeshi, diagonally to the right of Masachika.

"I knew we'd order the same thing, Masachika."

Yuki also had a bowl of mapo-tofu ramen, which belied her upper-class vibe.

"Wow, uh… I didn't know you ate stuff like that, too, Ms. Suou," stammered Takeshi nervously. Yuki took a hair tie out of her pocket and put her hair up into a ponytail with an awkward smile.

"You don't have to be so formal. It's not like we just met. We're classmates."

"B-but, like… Yeah, you're right."

"And of course I eat ramen. We don't eat it at home, but I often go out on the weekends for ramen."

"R-really? I guess I misjudged you."

Both Takeshi's and Hikaru's eyes were wide in astonishment after hearing how down-to-earth Yuki was, a departure from her ladylike image at school. She smiled even wider before elegantly beginning to

slurp her noodles. Masachika waited until she was eating and shot Takeshi a look.

You're way too nervous.

Speak for yourself. Maybe you are, but not me.

You wanna get to know her, right? How are you going to do that when you're trembling in your seat?

Sorry, but she's just out of my league.

Giving up already?!

As they conversed like this with their eyes, Yuki suddenly took a break from her ramen and exhaled deeply in satisfaction.

"This is really good, isn't it? I kind of wish it was a little spicier, though."

"Right? It needs more chili oil."

"I saw they had soy sauce and salt at the counter, but there wasn't any chili oil, unfortunately. The student council may need to have a talk about this during our next meeting."

"Way to abuse your power for self-gain," joked Masachika.

"I'm kidding," said Yuki, giggling.

Another unnoticed crease appeared in Alisa's brow as she quietly ate her lunch while listening to their friendly banter... The crease deepened until she eventually closed her eyes and consciously changed her expression.

"Are you two close?" Alisa casually asked.

"We're childhood friends, actually," said Yuki, grinning cheerfully after facing forward.

"Since childhood...?"

"We've actually been going to the same school ever since kindergarten. We've unfortunately never had class together, though."

"Oh..." Alisa nodded ambiguously, making it unclear if she was satisfied with Yuki's answer.

"What about you two? Are *you* two close?" asked Masachika. Alisa paused as if she didn't know the answer to that question, so Yuki decided to speak up instead.

"I guess you could say...we're still getting to know each other.

I want to be friends with Alisa, at the very least," she explained while gently smiling at Alisa and tilting her head. Alisa, wide-eyed, didn't quite know where to look.

With her eyes averted, Alisa gave an odd reply. "…There's nothing good about being friends with me."

Yuki blinked a few times, but a smile soon played upon her lips once more. "In other words, you aren't against the idea of us becoming friends, right?"

"Oh… Yeah, I guess?"

"Then let's be friends! We're both in the student council and the same grade, after all. Oh, hey! Do you think I could call you Alya, too? I always thought it was the cutest nickname whenever I heard Masha and Masachika call you that!"

"S-sure… Go ahead."

"Hee-hee! I can't stop smiling! You can call me Yuki or whatever you want, too, okay, Alya?"

"…Okay, Yuki."

Strangely enough, Alisa leaned away from Yuki, who was cheerfully giggling with her hands clasped together.

"I'm glad you two are friends now, but your ramen's gonna get soggy if you don't hurry," warned Masachika.

"Ah! I totally forgot about my ramen!"

Alisa watched with slight bewilderment as Yuki hurriedly ate her ramen; then she noticed that Masachika was staring, so she pouted awkwardly.

"So… Kuze… What have you been telling Ms. Su—Yuki about me?" she asked.

"Huh? Oh, nothing really… Just about how you always get mad at me and…that's about it."

"You make it sound like I'm always angry, but it's always your fault," argued Alisa as the corner of her eyebrows curled furiously.

"Can't deny that," replied Masachika, lowering his head as Yuki giggled.

"You don't have to feel embarrassed, Masachika."

"Hmm?"

"Masachika always speaks so highly of you, Alya. He told me you're a really hard worker and how he really respects you."

"...?!"

"I never said I respected her."

"But you still unconditionally show respect for hardworking people. Am I wrong?" replied Yuki as if she were some all-knowing, omnipresent being.

"..."

Masachika awkwardly looked away before facing forward once more, staring at Takeshi and Hikaru as if to say, "Come on, guys. Say something." Hikaru and Takeshi exchanged glances, gave each other slight nods, then simultaneously stood up with their trays.

"Well, we're done eating, so we should get going."

"See you all later."

Masachika tried to plead with his eyes as the two traitors started leaving.

Hey?!

Sorry, but I can't stomach any more of this.

I'm not comfortable around women for prolonged periods of time.

They then averted their gazes and hurriedly left the cafeteria, rendering all of Masachika's begging for naught. With his eyes, burning with resentment, locked on their backs, he suddenly heard Alisa whisper in Russian:

"<Hmph. Unbelievable.>"

When he turned around, Alisa seemed to be pouting, and yet she appeared to be somewhat happy as well. Noticing Masachika's stare, she immediately looked down at her food and quietly continued eating. Having finished all his ramen even to the last drop of broth, Masachika decided to simply watch her eat, but when she glanced up and noticed, she mumbled in Russian:

"<Stop staring at me, you jerk.>"

Alisa lowered her gaze even more while absorbing herself in her lunch, which made Masachika feel all warm inside.

Ohhh. She must be embarrassed after hearing that I respect her. Now I get it.

Nevertheless, he couldn't help but watch. It wasn't because he didn't understand Russian or was dense. He simply felt compelled to use his secret weapon.

"Huh? What was that, Alya?" he asked.

"By the way, Masachika…," chimed in Yuki, who still didn't understand the situation but could sense something was off, "…did you think about joining the student council like I asked?"

Alisa's chopsticks froze; Masachika rolled his eyes as if to say, "This again?"

"How many times do I have to tell you? I'm not interested. Besides, didn't you already get some new members the other day?"

"We did, but they didn't last long…"

This year's student council had started about a month before, in the beginning of June. The student council at this school was slightly unique because students ran as pairs for the positions of president and vice president, and the two elected got to decide who the other members were and what they did. Therefore, the number of members changed every year, and the current positions being held were president, vice president, secretary (Maria), accountant (Alisa), and publicist (Yuki). These were the only five members. In other words, there weren't any general members.

"I thought you said you were only going to allow girls to join this year, since horny teenage guys would keep anything from getting done. What happened to the three people you mentioned last time we talked? Don't tell me they all quit."

"They said they weren't good enough…"

"Oh…"

Masachika could understand how they felt. The mostly-female student council was incredible in more ways than one. It didn't help that the vice president and Maria were considered the two most beautiful girls in their grade, just like the two "beautiful princesses," Alisa and Yuki, who were also members of the student council. That alone would make any girl feel self-conscious, and yet to make matters even worse, Alisa was at the top of her grade, and Yuki used to be the president of the student council in middle school. Having to see someone better-looking and more talented than you every day would be hell for any girl. Even a guy joining the student council with the intent of hooking up with one of the beautiful girls would feel disheartened and quit once he saw how much more capable they were than him.

"That's why I think you would be a perfect fit, Masachika. You're more than qualified, and I think you would work really well with Alya and me. Plus, you already proved you could do it when you were the student council vice president in middle school."

"…?!"

Alisa stared wide-eyed with shock at Masachika after hearing that tidbit from Yuki. He frowned.

"Kuze was the vice president?" Alisa asked.

"Yep. In middle school two years ago, I was the president, and Masachika was the vice president."

"Oh…"

"It was a long time ago, and I'm never doing it again," Masachika insisted.

Yuki smiled, though she was clearly vexed by Masachika waving his hand around in genuine disgust, and she tilted her head at Alisa, who was still staring at Masachika in astonishment.

"You might be surprised, but Masachika gets things done when he needs to…despite being like *this* most of the time."

"What's that supposed to mean? '*This*'?"

"Hee-hee! I wonder that myself sometimes."

Alisa pouted while listening to their friendly banter. She seemed bothered.

"<I know he can. Hmph.>"

But her Russian whispers didn't reach their ears.

◇

"Anyway, I need to stop by the student council room before class."

"Oh, okay. See you after school."

"Yes, see you after school."

"Later, Yuki."

"Please give my proposal some thought, okay, Masachika?"

"It's not happening!"

"Ha-ha-ha."

"Hey! What are you smiling for?"

"Oh, no reason. Have a good day."

After leaving the cafeteria, Yuki bowed gracefully and walked away while Masachika crudely waved her good-bye.

"You two sure are close," commented Alisa, her voice 20 percent colder and more piercing than usual.

"Is that surprising?"

"Yes, very. I can't believe you have a female friend," sharply jested Alisa, causing Masachika to raise an eyebrow.

"Wait. *That's* what surprises you?"

"Yes, and?"

"I mean…" Masachika looked at Alisa as if she had two heads, then he pointed at her. "You. You're a female friend."

"…"

She slowly blinked, her expression blank, and tilted her head inquisitively.

"…We're…friends?"

"Huh? We're not, then?"

"…"

Alisa fell silent for a few moments, seemingly taken aback by the unexpected question before suddenly turning to face away from him.

"No, we are. We're friends," she replied flatly as if she was holding something back. She then immediately headed in the direction Yuki had gone.

"Hey! Where are you going?"

"I just remembered I had to stop by the student council room as well… Don't follow me," she succinctly demanded without even looking back as she left.

"What was that all about? …Eh. Whatever. More importantly, I need to make those two pay for running away earlier…," Masachika ominously mumbled to himself and returned to his classroom alone.

There were rumors that afternoon that some students had seen Princess Alya skipping down the hallway and humming to herself, although those rumors never reached Masachika.

CHAPTER 3

Yes, Officer. This man right here.

Masachika arrived at school the next day an hour earlier than he usually did. It wasn't for any special reason. He merely woke up an hour earlier than normal. It was unusual for him to feel so refreshed first thing in the morning, so he decided to go straight to school. He didn't want to risk falling back asleep and not being able to get up in time for class.

There was another small reason he came to school early, though. He just so happened to be on homeroom duty today. Not only were students seated at this school by their school number, but it also determined homeroom duty, which students did in pairs with the classmate sitting next to them. In other words, Masachika was going to be working with Alisa today.

Although he acknowledged he was lazy, he always took care not to inconvenience anyone (asking Alisa to show him her textbook when he forgot his didn't count as far as he was concerned). Therefore, he never skipped school when he was on homeroom duty, regardless of how boring cleaning was to him. Usually, only doing the bare minimum of what he was asked to do was what made Masachika who he was, but today was slightly different.

"Hmph. I impress even myself sometimes." Masachika nodded with evident satisfaction as he surveyed the empty classroom from the teacher's podium. The seats and desks were beautifully aligned, with each student's notebook lying neatly atop their desk after having been checked by their homeroom teacher. There wasn't a speck of chalk dust on the blackboard, and the erasers had been perfectly cleaned as well.

Alisa typically did this on her own during homeroom duty; it wasn't a requirement. But since he got up early today, Masachika wanted to see Alisa's expression when he said, "Huh? Oh, you mean the things you usually do? Yeah, I already finished all that." Thus, he returned to his seat and waited for Alisa to arrive early as she usually did. Only a few minutes had gone by when Alisa finally arrived. The moment she opened the classroom door and saw Masachika, her eyes widened in disbelief.

"Yo, yo, yo. Good morning."

"...Good morning, Kuze."

Alisa furrowed her brow as she looked around the room and realized that her usual tasks had been completed in their entirety.

"I woke up really early today and had a lot of free time, so I thought I'd clean the place on my own." Masachika looked cocky.

"...*You* got up early? I need to go outside to check if pigs are flying."

"Ah, Alya. You've always had a way with words."

"You'd better not fall asleep during class."

"...I'll see what I can do," was Masachika's half-hearted response.

Alisa rolled her eyes and sighed, then said quietly yet resolutely, "...I'll take care of the blackboard erasers after our morning classes are over."

Masachika smirked. It was clear she simply didn't want to feel like she owed him anything. In no way was that what he was trying to do, but after getting to know her over the past year, he realized Alisa was a proud person, and there was nothing he could say to change her mind.

"All right. Thanks," he replied.

Although she still seemed somewhat discontent, she nodded and awkwardly shuffled over to her seat. Curious as to why she was walking like that, Masachika eyed her up and down until he noticed her knee-high socks were wet, but one look out the window made it evident that it was a bright and sunny day. It had rained last night, but there wasn't even a dark cloud in the sky anymore.

"What happened to your socks? Step in a puddle or something?"

"Please, I'm not as bad as you."

"What kind of idiot do you take me for?! You think I'm a twenty-four-seven space case or something?!"

"I never said that... *Sigh*... Anyway, a truck passing by splashed water on me."

"Oh man. That sucks."

"I suppose it's kind of my fault for walking too close to the side of the road, though. I have a spare pair of socks to change into, at least."

Even though she made it sound like she didn't care, she took a seat at her desk and cringed with disgust as she removed her shoes. She then placed her right foot on the corner of her chair and hastily began pulling off her socks in front of Masachika. Her radiant, slim, milky-white legs wrapped in white knee-highs were exposed in all their glory right before his eyes as they glittered in the sunlight coming in through the window. Her thigh faintly peeked out from under her skirt as the sock slid down her lifted leg. Once it was off, Alisa stretched her wet, bare leg out as if she was basking in newfound freedom. Masachika swiftly averted his gaze, feeling as though he was looking at something he shouldn't have been. Despite only watching her take off her socks, he felt a strange sense of guilt, as if he had been peeping on her getting undressed or taking a bath. Her beauty was nothing new to him, yet Masachika felt like he'd just remembered exactly how beautiful she was. His heart started racing.

"*Phew...*" Alisa exhaled in obvious relief after taking off her other sock and wiping her legs dry with a small towel that she always had on her just in case it rained. When she casually glanced beside her, she noticed that Masachika was awkwardly looking off to the side, averting his gaze. Alisa blinked in surprise—the typically carefree Masachika looked oddly flustered and embarrassed...and that made her smile. It was a sadistic, mischievous smile. She swiftly turned to face him and extended her right leg, skillfully grabbing and tugging at his pants with her big toe and index toe.

"Hey, can you go grab some spare socks out of my locker for me?"

"What?"

"I accidentally took these ones off before grabbing my spares, so now I can't go get them."

She crossed her left leg over her right as if to say, "Did I really even have to explain that?" Masachika quickly looked away before he could see too much, making his nerves even more obvious. Alisa's sadistic grin grew as she rested her chin on her hand with her elbow on the desk. Seeing her smile in amusement with the morning sun behind her was nothing short of picturesque. She was like a selfish princess who was enjoying watching her servant perform an almost-impossible task, or a cruel boss or sergeant who was being unreasonable with her subordinate.

Alya would probably look good in both a dress and a military uniform...

With his thoughts flying off in that direction, he stood up from his chair and then walked over to Alisa's locker in the back of the classroom. He glanced at her once more to make sure it was hers, then opened the locker door, revealing textbooks and a pencil case neatly organized inside. In the very back were a folding umbrella and some socks in a clear plastic bag. He grabbed the bag of socks, still with a lingering feeling of guilt, then promptly returned to his seat.

"Here."

He thrust the socks toward Alisa while glancing at her out of the corner of his eye.

"Good. Now help me put them on," she demanded, dropping a verbal bomb while casually leaning back against the window.

"Whaaat?!" shrieked Masachika, but when he turned to face her, she'd already lifted her right leg in the air for him. She was tilting her head smugly. Perhaps since they were the only two in the room, she made her amusement no secret.

"What's wrong with you today?"

"What? Me? What's wrong with *you*?"

"I'm rewarding you for getting my socks."

"Rewarding me? Uh... Maybe some people are into that, but..."

"Oh? So you don't want to?"

Alisa looked surprised as she crossed her arms and recrossed her legs.

"No, I want to!" shouted Masachika, swiftly turning his head at the same time to avert his gaze.

He was planning on following that up by saying, "You've had your fun, so could you stop messing with me already?!" However, before he could even say another word, he heard Alisa whisper in Russian:

"<I want you to, too.>"

When he glanced to his side, her once-mischievous smirk was nowhere to be found. She was playing with her hair while averting her gaze, a soft blush on her cheeks. The sight alone sent Masachika's mind straight into the gutter at full speed.

What were these bashful sweet nothings Alisa always whispered in Russian? Masachika had been pondering that question until he finally reached this conclusion: *Alya's a mental exhibitionist.* Alisa was a hardworking perfectionist. That was her ideal version of herself, so she was always her own harshest critic and tirelessly worked herself to the bone. Nevertheless, the more people suppress their urges, the more pent-up stress they have that they need to release—at least, that was what Masachika once heard somewhere. Therefore, he believed her bashful Russian whispers were related to that somehow. In other words, she would whisper something embarrassing in front of others and enjoy the thrill of being caught, just like exhibitionists when they walked outside in public without wearing any underwear. Namely, what Masachika was trying to say was…

It's okay, since it's consensual!

If his assumption was correct, then that would mean that Alisa was someone who enjoyed the thrill of exposing herself. In other words, she was happy, and Masachika was happy! It was a win-win relationship!

…It was easy to imagine what people might say if they heard his conclusion:

What kind of reasoning is that?

What's a mental exhibitionist?

I'm sure a lot of creeps believed what they were doing was consensual.

Be that as it may, there were, sadly, no mind readers who could slap some sense into him. Masachika was still hesitant, though. Even though he had her consent, it was in Russian. He wanted to get her consent in Japanese first.

"What was that?" he asked, facing Alisa with his mind completely in the gutter. She smirked provocatively and tried to play it off just like he expected she would.

"I called you a coward."

Masachika had been waiting for her to say that. He dropped his jaw while mentally raising his arms into the air as if he had won a boxing match. Alisa then giggled with contempt and recrossed her legs.

"Anyway, it's fine. I can put my socks on myself—"

"That won't be necessary."

"Huh?"

He promptly got on one knee before she could take the socks out of his hands. She blinked in confusion for a moment, but right as Masachika placed his hands on her right leg, her eyes opened wide.

"Eep?!"

Alisa awkwardly shrieked as she experienced the uncomfortable, ticklish sensation of someone running their fingers down her foot from heel to ankle. Flustered, she reflexively jerked her leg into the air and held down her skirt.

"Hey, stay still."

"E-excuse me?! …Hey?!"

Alisa slapped her left hand over her mouth to prevent herself from squealing while she kept pulling her skirt down with her right. Masachika gave her a look as if he was fed up, but his lips were curled in a smirk.

"What's your problem? I thought you wanted me to help you put them on?"

"I know…what I said…but…!"

"I couldn't just let you call me a coward like that and get away with it. My pride wouldn't let me."

"Wait…! I still need time to mentally prepare…!"

But Masachika didn't listen to her cries as he pinched the sides of the sock with both thumbs and slowly pulled it up her leg. A tingle ran down her spine as the sock made its way upward.

"Ahn…"

Once Masachika's thumbs grazed her thigh through the thin fabric…

"Wh-what do you think you're doing?!"

"Bfff?!"

Alisa suddenly swung her foot up, hitting Masachika squarely on the chin and sending his rear straight to the ground. The back of his head slammed against his own chair.

"…!"

"Ah! S-sorry. Are you okay?" asked Alisa, clearly concerned. She even forgot her embarrassment and upset when she saw Masachika curled on the ground and clutching his head in agony. He extended his trembling right hand and started tracing his index finger across the floor as if he was writing one last message in his blood before his inevitable demise. Nevertheless, there wasn't any blood on his finger, so he was merely tracing with his finger alone, and yet Alisa could clearly tell what he was trying to write. It was a simple four-letter word: *pink*.

"…?!"

She instantly held down her skirt as she blushed in anger and embarrassment.

"Ngh…! Tsk…!"

She seemed to be having trouble getting mad at someone writhing in pain on the floor. Unintelligibly grunting, she grabbed her other sock off Masachika's desk and swiftly slipped it onto her left foot.

"<I can't believe you! Jerk! Screw you!>" Alisa childishly shouted in Russian after ramming her feet into her school slippers, despite the fact that Masachika was in the middle of dying on the floor. Right as Alisa was storming out of the room, two female classmates walked in and hurriedly moved out of Alisa's way with their eyes wide open at the unusual sight.

"Huh? What was that all about? Princess Alya was screaming."

"That was Russian, right? What's going on? Has the princess gone crazy?"

They watched her storm off with their mouths agape before turning around and noticing Masachika rubbing the back of his head.

"Good morning, Kuze… What happened?"

"Morning… Nothing happened."

"Hey, Kuze… What happened to your head?"

"Oh, uh… I've just got this one zit that's been bothering me."

"Uh-huh…"

They eyed him with suspicion as they sat down at their desks, but Masachika pretended not to notice and pulled out his smartphone to text his sister.

> Sister dearest, I'm in trouble

She must have been in the car on her way to school, as the message was immediately marked as read and she quickly sent a reply.

> What is it, my dear brother?
> Don't freak out, but…
> Gulp

The next message he received was a sticker of an anime character trembling with fear, which only heaped on more pressure. Masachika's expression contorted with extreme regret as he typed his reply.

> I…might have a foot fetish
> I beg your pardon?! I thought you were a boobs man!

> I was, dammit! I had no idea I was into feet!

> Hmph... It's about time you recognized how amazing legs are...

> Yeah...

> Legs are mad underrated. Thick thighs save lives, but muscular antelope legs are hard to pass up, too

> You are indeed wise, my dear sister

> By the way, brother dearest...

> Yeah?

> Did you seriously message me just to tell me about your filthy new fetish? WTF

> Sorry

Masachika's face fell. It felt as if his sister had just dumped a bucket of ice-cold water on him. He put away his smartphone and placed his head down on his desk.

"What am I gonna do now?"

Even Masachika realized he had gone too far. He thought he should probably go apologize, but he knew how prideful Alisa was; a reckless apology would make things worse.

"Eh. Guess I'll just think about what to do when she gets back."

Alisa wasn't a child, after all, so he figured she'd be back to her normal self once she cooled off for a bit.

That wasn't what happened, though.

"Anyway, that's all for homeroom today. Oh, don't get up and bow. I have to go," hastily mumbled the homeroom teacher before promptly leaving the classroom.

Morning homeroom ended surprisingly early today. There were still five minutes left until first period. Even so, the first-year students in Class B did not stand from their chairs as they began to whisper something to one another. There was only one reason behind the homeroom teacher's early departure and the nervous energy that filled the room. It was because Princess Alya wasn't wearing her usual blank expression but was instead resting her chin on her hand with an elbow on her desk. She was clearly in a foul mood.

"H-hey… What's up with her?"

"I heard something happened between her and Kuze, but that's all I know."

"Makes sense. He's the only reason she'd be in a bad mood. What exactly did he do, though?"

"I heard Princess Alya screaming earlier."

"Seriously? What was she screaming about?"

"Beats me. It was all in Russian."

As speculation of all kinds spread like wildfire, Takeshi stealthily got out of his seat, crouched low, and made his way over to Masachika's side.

"Psst. H-hey."

"What do you want?" Masachika whispered back so that he didn't stand out.

"Two questions. Did you really piss Alya off? And did she really do an *enzuigiri* on you?"

"What the hell?!"

Alisa instantly shot him a piercing gaze, and he flinched. An *enzuigiri* was an attack where you jump-kicked the back of your opponent's head. Not even the worst children would try to mimic this wrestling move.

"Alya would never do something so dangerous."

"Y-yeah, I figured."

"All she did was somersault-kick me on the chin."

"That's still pretty messed up, dude."

Takeshi laughed bitterly, thinking it was a joke.

It's closer to the truth than you realize, Masachika thought with an ambiguous smirk.

"So? What happened to Princess Alya that made her so upset?"

"Uh…"

"Come on, I know you did something. Just fess up."

"Well… I guess you could say it was my fault?"

Honestly, it *was* his fault. He did something he shouldn't have. But if he admitted he touched her bare feet and ended up seeing her panties, he would be instantly put on school trial, where they would unanimously vote to execute him. Therefore, Masachika evasively dodged Takeshi's questions while racking his brain for ways to fix things with Alisa.

"Uh… Alya?"

He decided to apologize for starters. Masachika pivoted to his neighbor, Alisa, who was resting her chin on her hand and staring out the window. She turned only her eyes in his direction as she sharply replied:

"What do you want, Kuze? <You foot-fetishizing creep.>"

There were plenty of things he wanted to say about this new Russian title that had been bestowed upon him, but he couldn't say a thing, since he was still pretending he didn't understand the language. Then again, maybe it was for the best that he didn't tell her that wasn't possible because he was a "boobs man." The stock Alisa had in him would plummet, and every girl in class would be rushing to dump their Masachika stock as well.

But the more I think about it, the more I feel like I didn't do anything wrong.

Alisa's cold behavior toward Masachika slowly led him to think this way. It was Alisa herself who'd ordered him to touch her feet, and it was Alisa who'd gotten embarrassed and kicked him. Being shown her underwear was beyond his control, and while he probably shouldn't have told her what color they were as if they were his final words, he had simply been trying to show that he wasn't angry that she had resorted to violence. So Masachika was a little unhappy that he ended up looking like the bad guy. Be that as it may, he understood that men were usually the ones in a vulnerable position in situations like this, so he decided to apologize and keep the other thoughts to himself.

"I'm, uh… I'm sorry…about what happened and all that."

"...Hmm? Don't be. I'm partly to blame. Plus, I'm not mad anymore anyway."

Then why are you in a bad mood? Masachika wondered, perfectly in sync with his classmates, who collectively thought, *Yeah, that's a big fat lie.* It actually wasn't a lie, though. Alisa was genuinely not angry anymore. What she felt right now was the embarrassment of having her leg touched and underwear exposed. Furthermore, she was embarrassed at herself for asking him to help her put on her socks, even though his reaction *was* priceless. There were many other small things she was feeling embarrassed about, such as screaming like a child, for example. She just wanted to crawl under a rock, build a little soundproof room, and scream. She was merely putting on a facade to make it look like she was in a bad mood so her true feelings wouldn't escape her heart. Unfortunately, Masachika was far too inexperienced to understand the complex nature of a young lady such as her and was clueless. The bell eventually rang, and their teacher for first period came walking into the room.

"All right, kids. Let's get this class started. Let's see who's on duty today... Ah, Kuj—... Kuze. Go ahead. Get us started."

After checking the name on the blackboard, the math teacher took one glance at Alisa and immediately pointed toward Masachika without missing a beat.

I know exactly how he feels.

Every student in class—except one—shared the sentiment.

"...Everybody, stand at attention. Bow. Good morning."

""""Good morning."""""

Naturally, the tense atmosphere in the classroom continued after the awkward morning greeting. As expected, the sandman came to pay Masachika a visit, since he had woken up extra early that day, but not even he was brave enough to nap in an environment like this. Still, that didn't mean he was going to be able to pay attention in class, so he spent the entire time thinking of a way to improve the princess's mood.

"All right, then. I'd like to end class there if there aren't any questions... Kuze, wrap things up."

"Everybody, stand at attention. Bow. Thank you very much."

""""Thank you very much.""""

The math teacher left the room without looking in Alisa's direction even once. Masachika exited the room right after, then hurried straight for the vending machine by the emergency exit. After getting what he needed, he rushed back to the classroom and reverently presented it to Alisa.

"Princess, please accept this offering in exchange for your forgiveness for what transpired earlier today."

In his hands was a can of sweet red-bean soup with mochi... which had been number one in the *drinks nobody asked for* ranking for the past fourteen years at Seiren Academy. It was essentially extremely sweet liquid bean paste that would always leave you ridiculously thirsty.

Red-bean soup?!

Everyone in the classroom stared at Masachika like he had absolutely lost his mind and was trying to start a fight with the princess, but he knew...she drank this bizarre form of liquid diabetes from time to time.

"...Didn't I just tell you I wasn't angry?"

"Heh. I know. I'm simply apologizing out of respect."

"...Fine. I'll take it."

"It is an honor."

After he handed her the can, she pushed the pull tab in and downed it in one go. Everyone in the classroom shuddered.

"Thanks."

"Ah, allow me to dispose of that can for you."

"I can throw away my own garbage."

"I cannot have you trouble yourself with such a task, my princess."

"Can you stop talking like that?"

"A'ight."

Her tone was still prickly, but Masachika could tell she was in a slightly better mood, so he returned to his seat feeling nothing but relief...when he came to a sudden realization.

Oh, crap... I don't have my textbook for the next class.

Usually, he would turn to Alisa for help during a moment like this, but asking her to share her textbook could very likely put her in a bad mood all over again. And if that happened, he wouldn't be able to handle his classmates' disapproving glares.

Great...

Masachika was rifling through his desk and bag when Alisa shot him a suspicious glance. He immediately looked away to avoid her gaze and asked the girl sitting on the other side of him, "Sorry, but do you think I could look at your textbook with you?"

"Huh? Oh... Sure."

She must have read the situation, because she smiled and sweetly nodded back at him. Masachika then scooted his desk next to hers while thanking her before letting out a deep sigh of relief.

"<Cheating scumbag.>"

The air suddenly got colder with the sound of that Russian whisper.

The heck was I supposed to do...?

But his lamentations were in vain; the classroom remained tense for the rest of the day.

CHAPTER 4

What's wrong with a little sisterly love?

"I'm home," announced Alisa after opening the front door to her apartment. Her older sister, Maria, poked her head out from the living room and welcomed her with a cheerful grin as gentle as a flower. Unlike the usually expressionless Alisa, Maria was almost always full of smiles.

"Welcome home, Alya."

She approached her sister while smiling from ear to ear with arms wide open, then kissed her on her right cheek, then left, then right again before bringing her into a tight embrace. The sight would make *yuri* fans around the world squeal like pigs with delight.

"Hey, Masha."

Alisa patted her sister on the arm to get her to drop the passionate embrace, and while Maria did let go, she suddenly turned her smile into a disappointed pout.

"Come on, we're in Japan now. Call me *big sister* like they do here."

"Not happening."

Maria puffed out her cheeks even more at her sister's cold reply. In Russia, people would usually call their older siblings by their name, unlike in Japan, where they would call them *big brother* or *big sister*. Therefore, Alisa, being born in Russia, would call her sister by her nickname despite Maria's frequent requests to be called *big sister*.

"*Sniffle...* You can be so cold sometimes, Alya..."

Realizing her pouting face wasn't going to work, Maria put on an even more pitiful expression, but Alisa promptly looked away and sighed. This wasn't anything new, but she always felt bad whenever her sister made this face. That still didn't mean she would call her sister *big sister*, though. After all, she was more of the serious type, unlike her easygoing older sister. It didn't help that Alisa was taller, and they were only one year apart. She had even been the one to look after Maria over the years as if she were the older one. That was why Alisa hardly thought of Maria as her older sister.

Calling her big sister *would make it sound like I was dependent on her, to boot...*

There were other things Alisa might have been willing to call her, but Maria was not having it. At any rate, Alisa decided to ignore her sister as she took off her shoes and swapped them for her slippers, but Maria immediately tilted her head curiously and blinked a few times.

"Alya, are you in a bad mood?"

"No...?"

Alisa eyed Maria dubiously to hide how she was really feeling, but such tactics didn't work on her older sister.

"Uh-huh... Does it have something to do with him again? With Kuze?"

Alisa walked right past Maria and headed straight for the bathroom, aggravated by her sister's prying and the sparkle in her eyes.

"Nothing happened."

"You know you can't lie to me. I can read you like an open book. So...? What happened?"

Maria followed her sister around like a duckling and continued to pry. It wasn't until she made her way into Alisa's room, plopped herself down on a cushion on the floor, and begged that Alisa finally gave in. Alisa took a seat, still dressed in her school uniform, and confessed with aggravation:

"It really isn't a big deal, but...we had a little fight. That's all."

"Oooh! A fight!"

Maria's eyes lit up with joy, even though it wasn't the sort of thing one would normally be happy about.

"...What?"

"Hee-hee! It's not every day you get into fights, after all! And with a boy, too."

"Yeah, I guess."

"Wow... There's finally a boy who has braved the frozen tundra around your heart."

"What's that supposed to mean?"

Alisa furrowed her brow at her sister's vague implications until Maria replied with a knowing smirk:

"You like him, don't you? This Kuze boy."

"...Excuse me?"

Alisa sent her sister a piercing glare as if to clearly say, "What is wrong with you? Did you hit your head as a child or something?" before shaking her head with a sigh.

"I don't know where you got that idea...because there's nothing like that going on here. We're just..."

Alisa suddenly remembered the confused look on Masachika's face the previous day at lunch when he said they were friends.

"Yeah... We're friends." The memory made her smile with smug satisfaction. That made Maria's smirk grow even further.

"Oh, you are, huh? But why? I thought you hated laid-back slackers like him?"

"Because, uh..."

Maria's assumption was correct. Masachika was not very motivated and didn't take things seriously. He was just like the kind of people Alisa usually disliked. So why did she consider him to be a friend? Alisa began searching her memories for the answer.

"<And the winner of the award for excellence is...Team B!>"

The classroom filled with applause. There was only one person, a little girl, in the crowd who was biting her lip with her head down. It was Alisa. She was in the fourth grade at an elementary school in Vladivostok at the time. This was the moment she truly realized that she was different from the others, and it was all because of a research presentation her class did. The students in her class were put into groups of four or five, given a topic to research for the following two weeks, and asked to post their findings on a trifold presentation board that they would then present to the class. The topic for Alisa's group was *local jobs*. They had interviewed local shops and family businesses and learned about their lines of work. It was the sort of innocent, simple project typically done in elementary schools. However, Alisa had always put everything she had into her tasks, no matter what they were. She'd always had a strong fighting instinct, even at a young age, and had always strived to be the best. It was only natural that she would aim for the award of excellence, which was essentially first place for best presentation. Therefore, she put a tremendous amount of effort into the project in order to win. Every day after school, she interviewed local shops until dinnertime and ended up filling out an entire notebook after only her first week. She took every possible measure she could to make sure she was ready for the group meeting to discuss their findings. But when the day finally came around, she was astonished by what the other three group members said.

"<Oh, sorry. I didn't interview anyone.>"

"<This is a bakery. This is a clothes shop. Huh? What do they do? A bakery makes bread, and a clothing store sells clothes. Duh.>"

"<Sorry, I've only interviewed half of my shops so far. But we still have another week, right? It'll be fine.>"

Their research seemed totally half-assed from Alisa's point of view. Even if they were to combine their findings, they still wouldn't have half as much information as Alisa. But the fact that they expressed absolutely no appreciation or worry made her more dumbfounded than mad. What really made her angry was when the three of them looked at Alisa's notebook.

"<Ew. What is all this? It's just a stupid project.>"

"<This is way too detailed. Yeah, we're not going to use even half of this.>"

"<Alya... Do I have to read all of it?>"

They stared at her with astounded gazes and forced smiles as if they couldn't believe her.

Wait. I'm the bad guy here?

Right after that thought crossed Alisa's mind, anger began to well up from the pit of her stomach.

No, I didn't do anything wrong. All I did was take my assignment seriously. I shouldn't feel bad. They should feel bad.

She was instantly filled with rage and disgust, and she was still far too young to suppress those feelings.

"<Could you guys take the assignment a bit more seriously?>"

The sensitive elementary-school children responded defensively to her piercing gaze and hostile tone. It wasn't long before it developed into a full-blown argument. They were in the middle of class, so the teacher almost immediately stepped in to stop them, but that brief moment was enough to sour their relationship to the point that it was clear Alisa wouldn't be able to work with them any longer.

"<If you don't like how I'm doing it, then you do it!>"

It was this response from one of her male teammates that had pushed Alisa over the edge. She decided that she would use the final week to create the best possible presentation according to her standards. But there was only so much one person could do in a week, and she hadn't been able to finish the project with the amount of care she'd intended. And as a result, another team had received the award for excellence. Alisa could not understand why her classmates didn't take the project seriously. She could not understand how they could smile and laugh, not caring that they had just lost.

We wouldn't have lost if the others had worked as hard as me. In fact, we wouldn't have lost if I had just done the entire project all by myself from the very beginning! I'm not like them. I'm the only one who took my assignments seriously and put forth the effort. I'm the only one who wanted to win.

The moment Alisa realized this was the moment she stopped expecting anything from others.

Nobody is at my level. Nobody has the passion or motivation to do what I do. That is why I'm going to do things the way I want from now on. I'm not going to lose to the unmotivated. I'm not going to lose to people who didn't work for it. I'm going to reach new heights nobody has ever reached before while you all just fool around the whole day. I don't need anyone's help. I can do everything myself. If you are going to half-ass something or if you are only doing it because you must, then you are only going to slow me down.

Even after the years had gone by and Alisa had become slightly more skilled socially, her fundamental view had not changed. If anything, these beliefs had only grown stronger. Every time she saw how unmotivated or academically challenged her classmates were, her disappointment in her peers grew until one day, she started unconsciously looking down on others. Once she realized this, she distanced herself from her peers to avoid any unnecessary friction. It was a lonely world. It was the sort of loneliness only felt by someone who had been born with the talent and fighting instinct that made them different from everyone else.

After Alisa finished her second year of middle school, her father was sent to Japan for work and brought the family with him. Following her parents' advice, she ended up transferring to Seiren Academy, which was known as one of the best schools in all of Japan. She had vague expectations that she might finally be able to work among her equals and improve alongside them, but she was instantly let down after taking the school's proficiency and placement test. She was at the top of her class now. It was the first time she had been in Japan in five years, and she was a transfer student from abroad with absolutely no idea what the test was going to be like. And yet even with those disadvantages, she had been placed at the top of her class.

Huh... This is what they consider a high academic level? I'm all alone, even here.

Right as her heart was slowly filling with resignation, she met him. It was on her first day as a transfer student on the morning of April 1.

"Your Japanese is really good, Alisa. Did you use to live in Japan?"

"You're so pretty! I've never seen anyone with silver hair before."

"Hey, did you really pass that stupid-hard entrance exam for transfer students with ease?"

Her new classmates crowded around and made their curiosity no secret. Although she was a bit daunted by the attention, Alisa tried to handle the situation without being overly rude. Nothing good would come from getting close to someone when she would ultimately look down on them. She would only make them uncomfortable, and it would make her uncomfortable once she realized what she was doing. That was why Alisa was not planning on becoming friends with anyone.

"Oh, the first bell rang."

"Already? That was fast. Talk to you later, Alisa."

"Let's continue getting to know each other during the next break, okay?"

"Okay."

After watching her classmates sadly return to their seats, Alisa glanced at the seat next to hers.

"..."

Sitting there was a male student lying sprawled out over his desk as if he didn't have a care in the world, despite all the noise and excitement that'd been happening right by him. The boy's free-spirited nature piqued her curiosity, to say the least. Before she realized it, she was lightly shaking his shoulders. It was the first time she was the one trying to start a conversation with one of her classmates.

"Hey, uh... The bell rang, you know?"

"Mmm... Hmm?"

An ordinary, young male student with a blank look on his face slowly lifted his head. It was Masachika Kuze. Kuze and Kujou. They were assigned desks next to each other simply because their last names were close alphabetically. He turned his blank stare at Alisa, blinked several times, then tilted his head.

"Ohhh... You're the transfer student who spoke at the opening ceremony, right?"

"Yes. Alisa Mikhailovna Kujou. Nice to meet you."

"Right… I'm Masachika Kuze. Nice to meet you, too."

That was all he said before facing the front once more and stretching his back. A few moments went by before his eyes widened with realization, and he tapped the boy in front of him on the back.

"Yo, Hikaru. I had no idea you were here."

"Seriously? Takeshi is here, too, man."

"Oh, wow. You're right. I fell asleep, so I didn't even notice."

Alisa was somewhat taken by surprise to see him pleasantly chatting with his friend and showing absolutely no interest in her. Alisa knew that she was twice as good-looking as the average person, and she understood that good looks could be used as a weapon when building relationships, so of course she was conscious of improving her appearance. Although she didn't use any makeup, since it was against school rules, she still understood that she possessed a beauty that rivaled the average TV star. And while she wasn't interested in attracting the opposite sex, she understood that her appearance, especially her silver hair, garnered a lot of attention. That was why Masachika, basically the only person who didn't express any interest in her, made a significant impression. But she soon noticed something while watching him curiously. It wasn't that he was not interested in girls or other people. He was simply unmotivated about everything. He would forget his textbook. He would sleep in class. He would even panic and rush through his homework during the break only minutes before class started. He would try not to stand out during PE just so he could put forth as little effort as possible. There wasn't even a hint of motivation being emitted from his lifeless demeanor.

Even prestigious schools like this have a student like him, it seems.

Alisa completely lost interest in the boy who sat next to her after that. It wasn't until the school festival in September when that all changed. This would be the last middle school festival for the third-year students. While some of them were busy preparing for their high school entrance exams, Seiren Academy was an escalator school. This meant most students would automatically enter the academy's high school next semester, so there wasn't too much pressure to study hard.

In fact, Takeshi, who was on the school-festival committee, suggested that his class do something huge for their last school festival, so they decided to do a haunted house. They were only highly motivated in the very beginning, though. Everyone had been excited during the planning phase, but their motivation dropped significantly when they discovered how mundane and difficult actually putting the haunted house together was. Alisa recognized this and was fully prepared to take on most of the work.

"Ouch!"

Alisa was still in the classroom after school and had started making the costumes all by herself when she suddenly pricked her finger with the needle and dropped everything. As a drop of blood emerged from the tip of her finger, she placed it in her mouth, sanitized it, then applied pressure until it stopped bleeding. She then placed a bandage over the wound so as to not get any blood on the costume she was making. This wasn't even the first prick. She already had five bandages wrapped around her fingers because she was inexperienced at sewing. And yet she continued working as she fought through the throbbing pain. She wasn't going to let something as insignificant as this stop her. If she was going to do it, she was going to do it right. That was what gave her the determination to pick up the needle once more and continue her task.

"Oh, hey. I figured you'd still be here."

The door to the classroom rattled as it suddenly opened. It was Masachika, who had almost immediately disappeared after homeroom was over.

"Kuze... What are you still doing here?"

"Eh. You know me," he replied evasively, glancing down at the documents in his hands. Alisa curiously followed his gaze, but she couldn't figure out what the documents were.

"Anyway, Kujou, you can go home now. We can finish that up tomorrow with the others," he added with a shrug, which slightly annoyed Alisa.

We're not going to finish in time if you keep putting it off like that.

Besides, I wouldn't have to be doing this all by myself if everyone else actually helped.

"Don't worry about me. I'm going to work a little more on this before going home." Alisa sternly refused, letting her irritation get the best of her.

"Oh... All right. Cool."

After Masachika took a seat at his desk and his eyes wandered a bit, he scratched his head a few times and casually said:

"I talked to the handicraft club, and they agreed to help make the costumes, so we should let them take over from here."

"Huh...?"

"And check this out."

Masachika handed Alisa the documents he was holding while she sat in a daze.

"I got permission to use the boardinghouse. I figured if we made it into an overnight event, it'd help motivate our classmates who are kind of losing steam."

"...?! But how did you...?"

"I talked to the student council. I used to be the vi— Ahem. I know the former president, so I asked her for a favor."

Alisa shot him a quizzical gaze as he corrected himself, but Masachika continued talking before she could ask him about it.

"Anyway, I promised to have a few of our guys help the handicraft club with some manual labor, so they agreed to help us. There are plenty of guys eager to show off to all those girls, so I'm sure we'll be fine there. Now, about preparing for the overnight workshop... Well, I suppose Takeshi can take care of that stuff."

"Huh?"

"Anyway, just go home already, okay? There's no point for you to be working hard all by yourself like this."

Masachika's casual comment caused Alisa's pent-up emotions to instantly explode.

"There's 'no point'? Excuse me?"

Alisa was extremely stressed out after working so hard sewing, despite being a novice. She felt as if all her hard work was being made light of after Masachika, a slacker she looked down on, suddenly provided her with a solution. It tore down the barrier protecting her heart. Before Alisa realized it, she had slammed the half-made costume in her hands onto her desk, swiftly stood up, and glared sharply at Masachika.

"If I—! If I'm going to be a part of this, then I want to do a good job! I don't want to go to the school festival with a half-assed haunted house! And I don't want to compromise no matter what!"

Even Alisa realized she was mostly just taking her anger out on him, but she couldn't stop herself.

"But…but I know this is me being selfish! I know nobody takes things as seriously as I do! That's why I'm working twice as hard to make up for it! Are you trying to say I'm wrong for wanting to do a good job?!"

She snapped at him as she allowed her feelings to get the best of her. It was the first time she had done something like this since elementary school. She was expressing raw emotion—something she usually hid. Masachika's eyes widened before he bluntly replied:

"You're dumping all your effort in the wrong places."

"Huh…?"

Alisa was taken aback by his unexpected, straightforward objection. Masachika looked her right in the eyes and quietly continued:

"You don't prep for the school festival on your own. You work together as a team, yeah? If you wanna contribute something good, then you don't just give up all because no one else seems motivated. You think of ways to get them motivated, y'know?"

"…"

Alisa instinctively wanted to look away from his unwavering gaze and indisputable argument, but her pride would not allow her. Instead, she glared right into his soul as if she wasn't going to back down. Before she could say anything else, however, Masachika swiftly averted his own gaze.

"…Uh, I guess I could've phrased that better. Sorry if I upset you.

I know you've been working hard, and I'm not trying to downplay that at all."

"Ah…"

When Masachika slightly lowered his head, Alisa no longer knew what to do with her anger. He responded to her misdirected fury with an apology, leaving her raised fist with no place to go. But what strangely flooded her with emotions and took her breath away was that single phrase: *"I know you've been working hard."*

"…I'm going home."

Those were the only words she managed to get out before she grabbed her bag and briskly left the classroom.

I can't… I can't believe him!

She desperately tried to suppress her countless whirling emotions as she headed for the school gate…and she pretended not to notice the grief, regret, and the hint of joy in the depths of her heart.

The next day.

"All right, you punks! Who's ready to have some fun?!"

The meeting for the school festival began with Takeshi's over-enthusiastic holler. As his classmates stared at him in confusion, he excitedly explained that Masachika had gotten them permission to use the boardinghouse.

"We can prepare for the school festival during the day, then use the old schoolhouse at night to play a scary game of hide-and-seek! It will be like our very own private pre-pre-pre-festival party with all sorts of fun! Yeaaahhhhh!"

The classmates smirked at his untamed enthusiasm while saying things like "The festival's not for another week" and "It feels like this has more to do with having fun than actually preparing for the festival," but his excitement was contagious, and they became animated as well. It didn't take long for them to come up with a schedule for the day of the event, and even when the meeting finally came to an end, everyone was still eagerly hashing out the details. They were even more elated now than they were when they were first discussing what to do for the school festival.

Some time went by, and it was finally the day they needed to prepare for their night festival. The boys were working extra hard and quickly because they were looking forward to not only that night's activities, but a home-cooked dinner made by the girls as well. The boost in morale continued even after the night at the boardinghouse, and they managed to complete the haunted house at the level of quality Alisa was after. In fact, it was even better than what she could have ever imagined. In the end, their haunted house made more money than any other booth, and they were awarded for their hard work.

"Ah..."

"Thanks for all your hard work, Kujou."

The late-night celebration party had finally begun, and the students were folk dancing in a circle around the schoolyard. Alisa was heading to the school building as she walked by her dancing peers when she ran into Masachika sitting on the stairs. He was resting his cheek on his palm, a slight smile on his face as he watched the others dancing. Alisa followed his gaze to find Takeshi hitting on every single girl he could approach, while Hikaru, on the other hand, was being asked by girls one after another to dance.

"Ha-ha... Must be rough."

"...You're not going to dance?"

He raised an eyebrow and shrugged at Alisa's question.

"Hmm? Nah. I don't have a partner to dance with anyway. This school can be so old-fashioned at times. Folk dancing at the night festival? Who does that anymore? At least there's no campfire, too."

"...Mind if I sit next to you?"

"Hmm? Uh, sure... You're not gonna dance? I bet there's tons of guys who're dying to ask you. Oh, hang on—do you not know how to folk dance or something?"

"Rude. I used to do ballet when I was little, for your information.

I can do what everyone else is doing easily. I just didn't feel like dancing, so I turned them all down."

Alisa snorted with contempt and flipped her hair over her shoulder, then took a seat right next to Masachika.

"Oh... Sounds rough."

"Not really. I'm used to it."

"Uh-huh. Guess I should've expected as much from the solitary princess."

"What's that supposed to mean?"

Alisa furrowed her brow quizzically.

"What? You don't know? That's what everyone's been calling you lately," replied Masachika, a surprised look on his face.

"...Hmph."

"Uh...you don't seem too thrilled about that."

"I guess that's because I'm not."

"Why? Because they're pointing out how much of a loner you are?"

"No, that's not it. Also, could you not insult me for once in your life?"

"Sorry."

He flinched under her piercing glare.

"Struck out again," joked Masachika while pouting. Alisa sighed.

"It's the whole 'princess' thing that bothers me," she told him.

"Why? It's a compliment."

"Is it? It makes me sound like someone from a fairy tale who's never worked hard a day in her life."

"Oh, huh... Never thought of it that way."

"I admit I'm better-looking and more gifted than the average person, but I've never taken that for granted. Not even once. I don't like people thinking I was just born with what I've worked so hard for."

"Makes sense," agreed Masachika. "I won't call you that, then."

"Okay," she replied as if she didn't care. But after a moment went by, she turned to face him and added, "...Thank you, Kuze."

"Hmm? For what?"

"This might be the first time I've ever enjoyed myself after a school festival."

Preparing for school festivals had always stressed Alisa out. She always had to compensate for her classmates, and when the festivals were finally over, she felt more exhausted than accomplished. But this time was different. She had fun working together and preparing as a team. The sense of achievement she got from succeeding with her classmates was far greater than anything she ever felt when she succeeded alone. Although she was tired, she felt a sense of exhilaration as well.

"I was wrong," said Alisa, averting her gaze. "I probably would have never been able to enjoy the school festival like this if I had tried to do the entire project alone… I'm sorry for taking my frustration out on you." Masachika uncomfortably wrung his hands.

"Don't worry about it. Besides, all I did was a little extra paperwork. You and Takeshi still worked the hardest."

Takeshi was the one who had actually led his fellow classmates, but it was Masachika who had set everything up and encouraged Takeshi to do that. Plus, despite appearing to be an unmotivated slacker, he was the one who actually created the positive work environment and always made sure that everyone was okay. While Masachika himself may have claimed he didn't do much, Alisa knew that none of this would have happened without him.

"I can't 'not worry about it.' I want to apologize for snapping at you…and I want to thank you for everything you did. Is there anything in particular you want?"

"Something I want? Uh…"

"You can't say 'nothing.'"

"Mmm…"

Masachika racked his brain for a few long moments, since Alisa had just blocked his path of escape.

"I'm pretty sure I remember hearing that people in Russia called each other by their nicknames as a term of endearment, instead of just their first names. What was your nickname?"

"What? Why do you care all of a sudden?"

"Alesha? Wait. Aleshka? That sounds like a Russian pet name, right?"

"...Alya. My family calls me Alya."

"All right, then. You can thank me and apologize to me by giving me the right to call you Alya from now on."

"What? How would that be a reward of any kind?"

Masachika wore a nihilistic smirk as Alisa furrowed her brow in bewilderment.

"I'd be the only guy in school who could call the class idol by her pet name. Booyah!"

"Were you dropped on your head as a baby?"

"Sounds like we have a deal! Thanks!"

"Ew," she spit out with a disgusted look on her face. That was when one of the guys from the group of male students who had gathered around her suddenly spoke up.

"H-hey, uh... Would you like to dance?"

"Hey! Who do you think you are, bro?! I was here first! Alisa, I've always loved you! Please dance with me!"

"What the...?! Who do you think *you* are?! You're not the only one who feels that way about her! I..."

Six guys suddenly crowded around Alisa after the first student spoke up. It must have been time for the last dance, so they'd all mustered up the courage to ask her.

"I'm sorry. I can't dance."

"Don't worry about it. I'm a good dancer. I can teach you."

"*You?* I'm a way better dancer than him. Come on, you'd rather dance with me, right?"

"Who cares who's better? All you have to do is move your body to the beat!"

Despite Alisa apologizing and declining their offers, the male students showed no sign of backing down. But as they slowly closed in on Alisa, she narrowed her eyes and suddenly stood up.

"Do you people—?"

But right before the merciless words rolled off her tongue, someone suddenly grabbed Alisa by the hand and pulled her to the side.

"Sorry, but she already has plans with me. Come on, Alya," said Masachika as he walked toward the schoolyard while still holding her hand.

"Hey…?!"

Alisa tried to protest, only to quickly follow him in a fluster. Under normal circumstances, she would have pulled her arm away and slapped him, but to her own surprise, she went along without making a fuss. Alisa's heart was pounding. She couldn't take her eyes off Masachika's broad back in front of her. When she really thought about it, she realized that this was the first time someone of the opposite sex had ever held her hand and whisked her away.

Yeah… I'm just a little confused because this is the first time this has ever happened to me. It doesn't mean anything more than that!

Right when Alisa began convincing herself of that, Masachika stopped in an opening in the circle of students, and the last song suddenly began to play.

"You said you used to do ballet and could folk dance easily if you wanted to, right?"

"Huh? Oh… Yeah. And?"

He smirked provocatively as she tried to calm herself down.

"Then let's see it, *princess*," Masachika teased. His intentions were obvious considering their conversation from a moment ago.

"You've got some nerve challenging me. Good luck keeping up with me and not embarrassing yourself."

"Don't get so into it that you step on my foot, okay, Alya?"

"Hmph! Bring it on!"

Alisa arched her eyebrows and frowned at the aggravating, smug grin playing on his lips. While the last dance was usually reserved for couples, there was not even a hint of sweet love in the air as they provoked each other. They began to dance just like those around them, but Alisa's steps gradually began to deviate from the norm. She elegantly spread her long limbs as she effortlessly danced under the night sky of the schoolyard. Although she was moving to the beat of the song, what she was doing could no longer be called folk dance. Nevertheless, Masachika managed to unwaveringly follow her speedy movements. He wasn't dancing at the same level as her, but he wasn't being completely shown up, either. His movements were good enough to not get in her way, and he skillfully managed to keep her dancing from getting too wild as well. Their match ended up miraculously working as a dance because they had clearly defined roles. One of them was obviously the lead role while the other played the supporting role.

Oh, right… This is just the kind of person you are.

That was when it finally hit Alisa. This dancing and skillful maneuver defined Masachika. He was a paragon of self-effacement. He would help others, not himself. He hid in the shadows to make others shine. That was the kind of person Masachika was.

"Hee-hee… Ha-ha-ha!"

Before Alisa even realized it, she was smiling. She had been unconsciously enjoying the dance from the bottom of her heart, though she had started it as a competition. However, it didn't last long. The song soon came to an end, and their dance ended along with it. Alisa eventually let go of his hand and bowed, albeit reluctantly.

"Man, I'm impressed. It took everything I had just to keep up with you."

"I had a lot of fun."

Masachika blinked with a dumbfounded expression. He seemed shocked by her honesty.

"…Well, I guess I should be heading back."

"Oh? You're not going to escort me?"

"Give me a break. Do you know how jealous that'd make all the other guys? They'd kill me."

"Uh-huh… Thanks for letting me know."

Her lips curled into a playful smirk as she suddenly wrapped her arms around one of his.

"Hey?! What are you—?"

"Walk me back."

"You're asking me to die for you. You know that, right?"

"It's payback for calling me 'princess.'"

"Ack…"

His face hollowed with despair, and yet he began to walk with her arms wrapped around his without even attempting to break free, so Alisa smiled in the highest of spirits, having finally gotten the upper hand. It was only then that she realized what she was doing and began to blush, but her good mood drowned out the embarrassment. She was walking side by side with someone, and that made her unbelievably happy. As they headed down the short path to the school building, Alisa felt the vague sense of loneliness and alienation that she had carried with her ever since that day in elementary school slowly melt into nothingness.

And yet the next day…

"Morning, Alya. Sorry to ask you this, but could you share your Japanese textbook with me?"

…Masachika had returned to his ordinary, unmotivated self.

"…"

"H-hey, uh… Alya? What's wrong? You're staring at me like I'm a piece of garbage."

"Because you are."

"What the…?! That's harsh," Masachika shouted.

"*Haaah…*" Alisa sighed as if for show before suddenly looking away from him with a pout.

"<And to think he was so cool yesterday…,>" she whispered.

Masachika still didn't change after that. He continued to amaze Alisa in all the wrong ways, and yet you could always depend on him more than anyone when help was needed. He would consistently be there by someone's side as if it was nothing. His behavior seemed

bizarre to Alisa, who always saw others as competition, but she felt relieved as well. The fact that she didn't have to compete with or compare herself to him eased her mind. And ever since then, she found herself able to interact with Masachika without feeling like she had to prove anything. She scolded his lazy behavior and teased him because she was frustrated by how laid-back he was. She was almost annoyed by how he seemed to watch out for others as if he was a cut above the rest, so she opened up in Russian and laughed at his ignorance and the absurdity of it all. The days went by like this until one day…

"You fell in love! Awww! That's wonderful!" exclaimed Maria, clapping her hands together.

"Were you even listening to what I said? I didn't fall in love." Alisa sighed.

"What? That sounded like the beginning of a love story, no matter how you try to spin it."

"Stop twisting my words to fit your narrative. I told you we were just friends. Remember?"

"Yep. From friends to lovers. It's very common. Sah and I were the same. Right, Sah?" Maria snickered while gently smiling at the picture inside the golden locket she had just pulled out from deep within her cleavage. She was so in love that there were practically hearts popping out of her head like in a comic book. Alisa coldly glared at her sister, who had switched into her usual maiden-in-love mode.

"But, well… I do recognize his skills, and I trust him," admitted Alisa reluctantly, looking anywhere but at her sister. Maria nodded while she continued to admire her boyfriend's picture.

"Yeah, there's nothing cooler than a guy who gets things done in times of need. Sah's the same. I can still remember when he swooped in to rescue me from that dog—"

"If you're just going to gush about your boyfriend, then get out."

"Oh, Alya! You're so cold!"

Alisa turned a chilling glare on her sister, who was puffing out her cheeks.

"And for your information, I like people who are hardworking."

"You still have a lot to learn, Alya. He's usually so laid-back and low energy, but all of a sudden, bam! He shows you how much of a real man he is! That's a good trait if you ask me!"

"Sounds like we don't have the same tastes, because it honestly annoys me how much of a slacker he usually is."

Alisa began to ramble on and on about his character traits and failings:

"He forgets his books all the time, he sleeps in class, and he doesn't even seem to care when I tell him to get his act together! He always just laughs it off like it's nothing, and… Well, I guess that's why I can say whatever I want without having to care…"

"Right? In other words, your relationship is built on trust."

"What in the world makes you think that?"

"Because he won't leave your side, no matter what you say. Isn't that why you can talk to him without a worry in the world? And he is fine with whatever you say. That sounds like a relationship built on trust if you ask me."

Alisa was lost for words after her sister's unexpected, insightful comment, but she quickly recovered and argued back.

"No, it's nothing like that. I can scold Kuze without having to care because everyone in class knows he needs to be set straight. That's all… But I admit he's easy to get along with. Getting along with others doesn't mean you're in love with them, though, right? Besides, having feelings for others means…you want to go on dates together and kiss and that kind of stuff, right? I've never even thought about doing anything like that…," mumbled Alisa while bashfully looking away.

"You're so cute, Alya." Maria smiled gently and clasped her hands together.

"Are you making fun of me?"

"No way. Alya, listen. You don't have to go on dates, kiss, or do anything special. If you care about him, then simply talking to him or touching him would feel special," boasted Maria with her large chest puffed out with pride. Alisa's eyebrow twitched.

"Could you be more specific?"

Astonishingly, Alisa had taken the bait instead of simply ignoring her sister like she usually did, causing Maria to blink with slight surprise. She stared into the distance.

"Hmm... The easiest example I can think of is holding hands. You don't even have to do that. If it's someone you like, even the brief touch of your hands would make your heart race. It would make you blush and want to scream, but not because you don't like it. It fills you with happiness and...," rambled Maria as she excitedly explained what love was while staring at the picture of her boyfriend and bashfully shaking her head.

"It makes you blush and want to scream..."

Alisa quietly looked down at her legs, then slowly extended her right foot toward Maria.

"What's wrong, Alya?"

"Sorry. Do you think you could help me take off my socks?"

"Huh? Why?"

Maria blinked in bewilderment at the sudden, bizarre request, but after seeing the look on Alisa's face, she had a good idea of what was going on, and so she scooted across the carpet and placed a hand on her sister's leg.

"Hmmm..."

Alisa watched with a slightly stern expression as her sister smoothly pulled off her sock.

"All done. Uh...want me to take off your left sock, too?"

Maria quizzically pointed to the knee-high on Alisa's left foot.

"No. Just put my right sock back on," replied Alisa with a crease in her brow.

"What? Why?"

"Just do it."

"If you say so."

Puzzled, Maria slowly slipped the knee-high back on her sister's foot while Alisa's grimace gradually deepened.

"Okay, all done. So...?"

"..."

Maria hesitantly looked up at Alisa's face, but Alisa was simply frowning at her leg without even glancing in her sister's direction. Before long, she sighed and stood up.

"This isn't working, Masha. You're no help."

"What's that supposed to mean?! That hurts, you know!"

"Yeah, yeah. Are we done here? Because I need to change, so I need you to get out."

"*Sniffle...* Is Alya going through her rebellious stage? Is that what this is? Sah, what should we do? Alya's become a rebellious teenager."

With drooping shoulders and a miserable expression, Maria was then kicked out of the room. Alisa gazed back down at her right leg and slowly traced her finger across her bare skin, but embarrassment caused her to look up, where she was instantly faced with her faintly blushing cheeks in her full-length mirror.

"Hmm..."

Alisa frowned as if to deny the fact that she was blushing, then imagined a certain young man and, grimacing, whispered:

"<It's not that.>"

Her Russian whispers drifted off into the air before ever reaching another soul.

CHAPTER 5

Please don't fight over me!

"It's finally over. Come on, Hikaru. Let's go."

"Okay."

After homeroom was over, Masachika gathered his belongings and looked up at his two best friends. As it was after school hours, the classroom was very relaxed.

"Hmm? Takeshi, you're going to band today? What happened to baseball?"

"No baseball today. The schedule's a little irregular at the moment."

"Oh."

Takeshi and Hikaru played in the band club together, but Takeshi was also in the baseball club. His reasoning was very *Takeshi*. It was simple and showed just what kind of pervert he was: *"I'm gonna do both sports and music to double my chances of becoming popular with the ladies."*

"You going straight home, Masachika?"

"Yeah, I've got nothing else to do."

"You should join a club, then. You're a little late, but they'll still accept you."

"Rather not waste my time."

"Dude, you're only young once. This is your time to live."

Takeshi shook his head at his friend's laziness, then gazed up at the ceiling in an exaggerated manner.

"Clubs strengthen the bonds of friendship! The smell of mud, sweat, and tears after countless days of hard work together...and burning feelings of love as pure as the vast blue sky!"

"Friendships die due to differences in opinions... The smell of metal, blood, and tears after countless days wasted...and a burning jealousy as dark as night when the top players on the team steal all the girls for themselves."

"Quit it! Stop bringing up only the negative things! Our clubs are nothing like that!"

"Yes... Friendships are fleeting."

"See?! Look what you did to Hikaru! Now he's joined the dark side!"

"Sorry, Hikaru. I shouldn't have said that. Go enjoy your club."

"Love hurts far more than it helps..."

Masachika and Takeshi panicked as the light in Hikaru's eyes suddenly went out and his shadow darkened. After finally managing to purify Shadow Hikaru's tainted soul, Masachika said his good-byes and headed over to the shoe lockers.

"A club, huh...," Masachika muttered unenthusiastically as he watched the soccer club gather in the schoolyard.

Masachika had plenty of free time to join a school club now, unlike in middle school when he was extremely busy with the student council. It wasn't that he didn't feel conflicted when he saw his friends having fun in their clubs, but none of the clubs spoke to him. He didn't feel moved. Joining a club would be more of a pain in the ass than it was worth. Starting something new was exceptionally exhausting to Masachika.

"I'm probably going to keep letting opportunities slip by until I eventually end up doing nothing...," he muttered in self-deprecation. But all he felt was frustration. There was nothing that inspired him.

"Oh."

All of a sudden, his smartphone began vibrating in his pocket. After making sure there weren't any teachers around, he took out his phone and gazed at the message on the screen.

Masachika sighed softly before turning on his heel.

◇

After making his way down the hallway, he knocked on the door to the room he'd been asked to stop by, opened it, and met the eyes of Yuki Suou, the person who'd sent him the message. Yuki, who was squatting before the shelf and organizing the equipment, cheerfully smiled at him like a flower, held her skirt down, and stood up.

"Masachika! Come here, come here!" she proceeded to say in the sweetest of voices while running over to him. She put on a cute act and really played it up—far different from her usual elegant, ladylike self. If anyone else at school had seen her, they would have fainted in shock while wondering if she had eaten something funny, but Masachika simply smirked and played along.

"Sorry, my dear. I hope I didn't keep you waiting!" he shouted in a coaxing voice, prancing toward her as well. Yuki would most likely get a pass if caught in the act due to her beauty, but what Masachika was doing was objectively disgusting. At any rate, Yuki didn't seem to care, and she continued:

"Well, you did! I've been waiting for you for sooo long! ♪"

"Hey! You're supposed to say, 'Not at all. I just got here, too.'"

"You two sure are close."

Masachika froze the moment he heard the cold voice drifting from the other side of the shelf. His expression remained frozen. He looked in the direction of the voice, where he saw the blue eyes of a reproachful glare peeking between the gaps of the equipment stacked on the shelf.

"Oh, Alya. Didn't know you were here."

"Well, excuse me for being here."

"No, you're fine. Ha-ha…"

Masachika forced a smile at Alisa while sending Yuki a protesting gaze, but Yuki simply tilted her head to the side as if she had no idea what was going on and smiled gracefully like the gentlewoman she was.

You filthy little…

Masachika had a strong urge to flick Yuki's forehead in retaliation, but he knew he couldn't in front of Alisa, so he just cleared his throat and moved on instead.

"Ahem… So…? You wanted my help organizing the equipment?"

"Yes, it's far too much for us to do alone. Do you think you could help us?"

"Sure, I guess… I feel like I'm being used, though."

"It's just your imagination."

"Yeah, I'm not so sure about that."

Masachika and Yuki continued to joke around as they headed to the back of the room.

"Ready to get to work, Alya?"

"Ready," replied Alisa without even looking away from the equipment on the shelf. Masachika smirked while taking the equipment list Yuki handed him.

"Anyway, do you think you could start helping out with these?" Yuki asked.

"Desks and folding chairs… You want me to count them and make sure none of them are broken, right? Got it," Masachika replied. "By the way, this has been bothering me since middle school, but…is this really the student council's job?"

"I have no clue, but it really helps to have a good idea about the kind of equipment and supplies we have for events."

"I guess that makes sense, but this is way too much work for only two girls."

"The president is supposed to be here soon to help, but he's very busy, so who knows how much longer it's going to be."

"Ohhh. All right."

Masachika went straight to work, once again realizing just how understaffed the student council was. He made sure the number of chairs and desks matched the number written on the list while removing chairs that had ripped cushions, missing leg caps, and the like.

"I'm impressed. You've still got what it takes."

"Yeah, you know me."

Masachika made sure not to show how tired he was as Yuki

showered him with praise and Alisa gazed at him from behind with admiration.

Damn, my arms are starting to hurt.

It was clear to Masachika that he had way less stamina now compared with two years ago when he was working hard in the student council. His arms and lower back were already hurting from stacking all the folding chairs.

Oh gosh. I'm beat. This sucks. I wanna go to sleep. I should have never agreed to do this. I could have at least tricked Takeshi into helping if Yuki had sent me that message a few minutes earlier. Why even ask for my help if the president is supposed to come?

Although Masachika inwardly talked a lot of trash, he converted his complaints into energy and worked quickly.

"Masachika, do you think you could give me a hand?" Yuki suddenly asked from behind.

"Hmm?"

Masachika turned around to find Yuki pointing to a cardboard box on the highest shelf with a slightly troubled expression. Yuki was small even for a teenage girl, so it would be difficult for her to lower a box off the top shelf all by herself.

Now it makes sense. She needed me to help with all the heavy lifting and grabbing stuff in high places.

He walked over, stood a bit farther down than Yuki, and lowered the cardboard box from the top shelf onto the floor.

"Thanks, Masachika."

"No problem… Hmm? What are these?"

After catching a glimpse of small colorful boxes under the slightly ajar lid, Masachika curiously opened the cardboard box to find multiple tabletop games inside.

"Card games, board games… What is all this?"

"It apparently used to belong to the tabletop club before it disbanded a few years ago. So now it's the school's property, since the club bought all of it with their budget."

"Oh… So the school's still lending this stuff out?"

"Yes. Most students have no idea these games even exist, though."

"No doubt about that. When would anyone even use them?"

"Maybe for their booth during a school festival? Or for a club party, perhaps? I actually played a few games with the new student council members at the welcome party the other day."

"Oh? Who won, by the way?"

"Uh… I ended up winning, I suppose."

"Figured."

"And second place?"

"Less talking, more moving, you two."

"Oh, right. Sorry, Alya."

"My bad."

They straightened at Alisa's scolding, ended their conversation, and returned to their tasks. The only thing on Masachika's mind after that was work. Silence reigned over the room for the next long few moments. Only the sounds of boxes being moved and pencil lead scraping paper could be heard until Alisa whispered in Russian:

"<Pay attention to me, too.>"

Masachika took a critical hit to the heart! It was a surprise attack, which made it super effective!

Ahhh! Wait. No. This is just Alya flashing! She's just flashing me verbally! I can't react!

Masachika clenched his teeth, desperately fighting against the irritating tingles running down his spine, while Alisa simply enjoyed the thrill. She enjoyed saying something embarrassing with the thought that no one would ever understand her. In other words, this wasn't how she really felt, and reacting to what she said would only make things worse!

"<Pay attention to meee! Look at meee! Talk to meee!>"

The pressure was on!

Masachika could barely stand it as he listened to her endless sing-song whispers. It was to the point that he couldn't deny that this was how she really felt anymore.

How can she even say all that?! Is she seriously not embarrassed?! Masachika mentally screamed, but it wasn't as if Alisa wasn't embarrassed, either.

Hmm?!

Alisa inwardly groaned in agony. Her heart raced for more reasons than one as she crouched in front of the shelf and tended to her tasks, constantly glancing at his back, despite thinking he didn't understand. But she felt relieved every time she saw him going about as if nothing was wrong.

H-heh. He has no idea, even though I'm making it so obvious... H-hmph. Take a hint, jerk.

They worked back-to-back while trembling in embarrassment. It was a humorous sight from an outsider's perspective.

"<Pay attention to meee! To meee!>"

Ack! N-no, I'm not going to lose! There's still no proof that she's even talking about me, either! Maybe she wants Yuki to pay more attention to her...

"Alya, is everything okay?" Yuki asked from nearby the door, even though she hadn't noticed their weird behavior. Alisa's heart skipped a beat, but she still promptly managed to change her expression and tone.

"Oh, sorry. I was just singing a little song.

"<I wasn't talking to you.>"

Aaaaand it's me! I knew it, but I didn't want to admit it!

The relentless three-hit combo almost knocked Masachika out cold, and his knees trembled.

"O-oh, a Russian song, huh? What's it called?"

Alisa swiftly turned around and looked at him. Maybe it was only his imagination, but she seemed a bit happy as well. Regardless of the truth, the thought alone did a lot of damage to Masachika.

"It's called..."

"You forgot what it's called?"

"No, I remember. It's called...'A Feeling Gone Unheard'?" bashfully replied Alisa with hooded eyes.

"Oh…"

Masachika died.

"Well, that should do it. Thank you so much for helping us, Masachika."

"Thanks."

"No problem."

About an hour after starting, Masachika had emptied his mind and detached himself from the physical world, which helped him speed up his work considerably. The three of them finished organizing far earlier than expected, but when they left the supply room, they were approached by a large male student.

"Oh, you're done already?"

"Oh, if it isn't the president. Yes, we finished earlier than expected thanks to Masachika's help."

"Awesome. So you're Masachika Kuze, huh? I'm the president of the student council, Touya. I've heard a lot of good things about you."

"Uh-huh. Nice to meet you, too."

Masachika bowed, then looked up at the guy. He didn't need to be introduced because he already knew who he was. His name was Touya Kenzaki, and he was a second-year student and the charismatic president of the high school student council. He was a large guy but not just in height. He had broad shoulders and a thick chest, so he looked even *bigger* close-up. He wasn't the best-looking of guys. If anything, he seemed old for his age; this, coupled with his large stature, made it hard to believe he was still a high school student. However, his eyebrows were well groomed where they hung over his stylish glasses. But what stood out most of all was his extremely confident expression, which gave him both charm and a strong presence. Just one look at him would make it clear that he was someone you could count on. That was why everyone naturally felt they would be okay with him in the lead. Perhaps rulers such as kings had a regal presence like his. Most guys at school had extreme doubts at first when they heard that one simple guy was leading four beautiful, talented girls all by himself, but everything made sense the moment they saw him. Masachika honestly felt the same way.

"Well, I need to get going."

"Hey, wait. I'd feel bad sending you home without thanking you somehow for helping. I know you need to get home, but let me treat you to dinner."

"I appreciate the thought, but…"

Masachika was hesitant. Of course, he was uncomfortable being treated to dinner by someone he had just met, but he also had a bad feeling in his gut as well. He wondered if perhaps this was what Yuki was really after when she asked for his help.

"Why not take him up on his offer? It's not like dinner is waiting for you at home, right?" chimed in Yuki as if to confirm his suspicions.

"Yuki…"

"Hmm? How would you know that?" asked Touya as he and Alisa stared at them in utter bewilderment.

"Because we're childhood friends," said Yuki with a straight face.

How does that explain anything?

Masachika—and probably Touya and Alisa as well—thought that, but the overwhelming power behind Yuki's archaic smile kept them from saying anything.

"Okay, then… That's all the more reason for us to go grab something to eat. Alisa, Yuki, you're coming, too. I want to thank you two for today as well."

"Thank you very much."

"…Right. Thanks."

"If you say so."

Before Masachika even realized it, it had been decided that the group was going out to eat. While he wasn't thrilled about it, he didn't feel like arguing over it, either, so he hesitantly went along.

So this is the power of the president…

While inwardly sighing, Masachika casually turned to his side to look at Alisa.

"...What?"

"Nothing."

"Excuse me? You know it's rude to stare at a lady's face for no reason."

"Sorry."

He looked forward and reflected on his behavior, since she was completely right.

And this is the cold, heartless accountant of the student council...

Thinking about such nonsense, Masachika began to daydream.

"<You're going to make my heart race if you keep doing that.>"

Masachika nearly died again, but he continued to stare forward. He could sense Alisa grinning and glancing in his direction, but he didn't have the capacity to respond. He was already long out of MP. He returned to emptying his mind while slipping into his shoes at the school entrance and then stepping outside. That was when they ran into the soccer club, which most likely had just finished practice, but the athletes naturally moved to the side the moment they saw the four of them.

They aren't moving out of the way for me. That's for sure.

Even as they passed by, the soccer club members' eyes were glued to them, especially Alisa. Yuki was the next in line for most stares, followed by Masachika, who was only being looked at because they had no idea who he was. It was as if their eyes were saying, "Who the hell is this guy?"

Can't blame them.

Even though Masachika himself realized that he didn't belong there, it still didn't help how uncomfortable it made him. However, neither Alisa nor Yuki batted an eye, despite being gawked at. They didn't seem to care. When they left the school, the environment changed, but the situation did not. Even people merely passing by couldn't take their eyes off the two girls, but everyone except Masachika seemed to be completely used to it. They walked down the street for around ten minutes until they reached a restaurant. Touya was the first to sit down after they were led to a table, so Masachika urged the other two to go ahead so he wouldn't have to sit across from him. However...

"Here, Masachika. Have a seat." Yuki innocently smiled while offering the seat right in front of Touya.

"You heard the lady, Alya," said Masachika, feigning ignorance, as if he was throwing her a hot potato.

"She was clearly talking to you."

The stalemate continued for the next few seconds until Touya finally broke the silence.

"Come on, just have a seat, Kuze. The waitress is waiting to take our order."

When Masachika glanced to his side, a waitress was idly waiting with a tray carrying four glasses of water, so he gave up and plopped himself down in the seat in front of Touya. Yuki then smoothly slid into the seat by his side while Alisa sat next to Touya.

"I know it's a little late to bring this up, but isn't it against school rules to wear our uniforms off campus?"

"Don't worry about it. We often go out to eat like this when the student council works overtime like today. Plus, it's an old rule that nobody follows anymore anyway. So just order whatever you want and enjoy yourselves. Keep it within five thousand yen, though."

"I thought you were really cool up until that last sentence, President."

"Heh! It's not the wallet that makes the man, Yuki."

Touya's playful response broke the ice, helping Masachika to relax as well. But it was still too early to let his guard down. Everyone ordered, keeping their meal under a thousand yen per person, and Masachika soon became the topic of conversation.

"Anyway, I'm still surprised you managed to organize everything that quickly. I totally thought it was going to have to be finished tomorrow," stated Touya.

"We wouldn't have been able to do it without Masachika's help.

Having a man around really makes a difference, especially one who's used to this kind of work," Yuki immediately chimed in.

"I bet."

"Masachika is incredible. It doesn't matter if it's physical labor or desk work. He gets the job done without even a single complaint. And he's quite the negotiator, to boot."

"Yuki, stop making me sound way better than I am. You're overselling me."

"It isn't often Yuki speaks this highly of someone, though. What do you say? Interested in joining the student council? We actually don't have any general members to help us out."

Masachika was not surprised in the least that it had come to this. After glaring hard at Yuki beside him, he replied:

"I'm sorry, but I'm not interested in joining the student council. I already had my fill in middle school, and I'm done."

"Hmm… While I admit things in the student council are a bit more intense in high school, it's much more fulfilling as well. We're given a lot more freedom to make decisions compared with other schools, and to be blunt, it positively affects our transcripts."

Touya was just being truthful. Simply being part of the student council at Seiren Academy put one in an extremely beneficial position. Not only would it give them advantages for getting into university, such as positive letters of recommendation, but the positions of president and vice president were also elite titles that went beyond the usual school pecking order and held significant meaning after entering the workforce. There were even social gatherings solely for people who used to be the president or vice president of the student council at Seiren Academy, an institute known for producing impressive graduates who went on to work in politics, finance, and elite business establishments. If you could function as a member of the student council for a year, then it was essentially guaranteed you would succeed in the workforce as well. Conversely, if you did a poor job managing and caused a major problem, then you would be labeled *incompetent* for the rest of your days. Yet in spite of that, there were still countless people who fought for the position of vice president and president. Furthermore, the quickest way to work your way up to those positions was to become a general member of the student council first.

"Sorry, but I just don't have the ambition. I don't plan on going to a different university, and I'm not really interested in making connections with big shots after graduating, either."

But none of that was enticing to someone who didn't have any specific dream for their future and idled the days away like Masachika.

"Come on, don't be like that," said Yuki. "Let's join forces. Let's run together."

"Seriously? You're *already* asking more from me? Besides, you don't need me. It's pretty much guaranteed you're going to be elected president next election cycle, right? You were president in middle school, after all."

"I want to run the student council with you, Masachika."

"No way. It's too much work."

Over 90 percent of the guys at school would agree to help Yuki without even giving it a second thought, but Masachika continuously turned her down. Touya stroked his chin while watching them in amusement.

"Masachika. Yuki isn't guaranteed to win, just to let you know. There are plenty of other candidates, including Alisa here," mentioned Touya before glancing at Alisa by his side. When Masachika instinctively looked over at her as well, his eyes immediately met hers.

"Alya? You plan on running for president, too?"

"Yes, I am going to run against Yuki next year."

Alisa looked over at Yuki, who was smiling calmly, but Masachika could practically see the flames roaring behind the two girls.

"By the way, Alisa, you sit next to Kuze in class, right? What do you think of him?" Touya promptly changed the subject to lighten the mood, but he ended up only adding gasoline to the fire.

"What do I think? Honestly, I can sum him up in one word: *uncommitted*."

"Oh?"

Touya appeared to be greatly interested in Alisa's heartless remark. He then glanced in Masachika's direction, but Masachika simply shrugged because she was right. In fact, he was actually thinking, *Yeah, that's the spirit. Yuki talked me up so much that I need someone to bring me down.*

"He always forgets his textbooks, he barely pays attention in class, and it would be faster to count from the bottom if you want to know where he stands with his grades."

"At the very least, he does do the bare minimum, so he isn't failing any of his classes," explained Yuki as if to balance out Alisa's relentless critiques, causing one of Alisa's eyebrows to twitch and the flames behind her to reappear.

"...Yes, I know he's passing his quizzes, since I'm the one grading them. He manages to get good enough grades on them to avoid having to take the makeup quizzes, and I can somewhat admire that, but he could do so much better if he applied himself."

"Masachika has always been really smart, after all. He got into Seiren Academy even though he barely studied for the test. Oh. Of course, I only know this because we grew up together."

"Kuze's really athletic, too, but he's hopeless when it comes to ball sports for some reason. He even jammed his finger playing basketball in PE the other day."

"He's always been bad at ball sports, ever since we were little. I'm not any better, though. Masachika's favorite sport in PE was always long-distance running."

Whoosh! The imaginary fire behind Alisa roared higher. Masachika literally began to sweat, despite it not actually being hot. It was even stranger since Yuki had the calmest, coolest look on her face.

"S-sorry to keep you waiting," hesitantly squeaked the waitress carrying their food. She forced a diplomatic smile as the two young girls sitting by the aisle continued to emit an alarming aura. She appeared to have been holding the tray for quite a while, sadly enough. Today was not her day.

"Oh, great. The food's here. Let's eat."

Those simple words from Touya ended Alisa and Yuki's staring contest and restored peace to their table—much to the waitress's relief—sending Masachika's respect for him through the roof. Touya, however, already had a girlfriend, so naturally, none of this would ever develop into love.

After finishing their meal, they left the restaurant and discovered that it was already dark outside. The rest of the conversation during dinner was peaceful, since Touya, the host, led the discussion for the most part and Yuki, who had strong communication skills, would back him up and keep things moving. Masachika and Alisa were exclusively listeners, so while there were no conflicts, that was all that could be said for them. During that conversation, both Touya and Yuki repeatedly invited Masachika to join the student council, but he refused each time.

""""Thanks for dinner.""""

Masachika, Yuki, and Alisa offered Touya their thanks after Touya finished paying for the meal and joined them outside.

"No problem." He nodded, then began to lead the others toward the parking lot while wearing a thoughtful expression. "I know Alisa lives nearby, so she walks home, and Yuki is taking the train back like me, but what about you, Masachika?"

"Oh, I can walk home from here, too."

"All right. Then walk Alisa home on your way. I'll take care of Yuki."

"Okay."

The fact that Masachika promptly agreed like a gentleman, as if it was only natural, made their respect for him grow even more. Yuki, however, suddenly raised a hand.

"Ahem. President? I really appreciate the thought, but I already have a car coming to pick me up."

"You do?"

"Yes. I need to wait here until it arrives, so please don't worry about me."

"…Okay. See you next week, then."

After seeing Touya off as he walked down the road toward the station, Masachika's and Alisa's eyes met.

"Ready to go?"

"You don't need to walk me home."

"Come on, don't be like that. Let's go. Later, Yuki."

"Have a safe trip home."

"See you later, Yuki."

"See you, Alya."

Masachika and Alisa began walking in the opposite direction Touya left in, and Yuki gave a small bow in farewell.

"How far's your place?"

"It's about a twenty-minute walk."

"Oh. That's kinda far."

"What about you?"

"Me? Around fifteen minutes, give or take a few. It probably isn't too much farther than your place depending on how fast you walk."

"Oh."

Then there was a hush. They walked in awkward silence until the door to a local chicken-skewer joint a little way up ahead opened and a group of men in suits came busting out.

"Tsk. The guys in development have absooo-*lutely* nooo respect for us in sales!"

"I think you've had a little too much to drink, Boss."

"Mr. Isoyama, we should probably keep our voices down."

A middle-aged man with glassy eyes and a bright-red face babbled drunkenly and loudly as his subordinates tried to calm him down. Masachika moved Alisa to the inner edge of the sidewalk to let the obviously intoxicated individuals pass by. Although he made sure not to make eye contact, the man they had called Boss suddenly caught sight of them while he was passing by. He immediately grimaced with disgust as if something about them bothered him and raised his voice:

"What the hell? What are these kids doing out this late? Banging? Ya gonna go hit that? All kids wanna do these days is fool around! Ya should be back home studyin'!"

"Mr. Isoyama! Shhh!"

"That's enough, Boss. Let's go home."

"Shaddap! Look... The hell is that?"

The man crossed into their personal space, ignoring his men's pleas, and stared hard at Alisa before letting out a snort.

"What are ya, a little gray rat? What kind of dirty hippy parents let their daughter dye their hair like this? What a disgrace!" shouted the middle-aged man, making sure everyone could hear. Alisa immediately stopped in her tracks.

"Alya, hey..."

Recognizing Alisa's fury, Masachika urged her to ignore the drunk so they could avoid any trouble, but she shot the man a cold, piercing gaze.

"Embarrassing for a man your age to act like this," barked Alisa with unrivaled contempt. Though her voice was small, it rang out clearly among the boss's and his men's shouting. Every businessman there froze in mute amazement, but their boss's expression quickly twisted into rage. He pushed his men away and stomped over to Alisa. She turned to face him as well and stood strong, showing no signs of retreating, but before he could get in Alisa's face, Masachika swiftly slipped in front of her, smiling so sweetly that it was hard to believe a clearly enraged man was approaching them.

"Long time no see, Mr. Isoyama. I haven't seen you since my brother's wedding."

"O-oh, uh... Yes?"

The man was caught off guard by the sudden polite greeting and stopped in place. Bewilderment clouded his face while he stared at

Masachika as if the unexpected turn of events had sobered him up a little.

"I'm glad to see you're doing well. My brother told me what incredible business partners you all have been, so it left a really strong impression on me."

"O-oh, yes. Of course." The man nodded, even though his expression made it clear he had no idea who Masachika was. Nevertheless, the words *business partners* were enough to make him start to panic. As the other businessmen and Alisa watched in confusion, Masachika continued, still with a gentle smile:

"Now that I think about it, you drank a lot during my brother's wedding as well. You really love to drink, huh?"

"Oh yeah. I live for drinking on the weekends like this. Ha-ha-ha!"

"I bet. Oh. By the way, this is my fiancée," boasted Masachika with a laugh as he placed a hand on Alisa's shoulder. She stared wide-eyed at Masachika, mystified by the unimaginable turn of events. "She is an incredibly smart woman. I'm just lucky to have her."

"Oh… Yeah… She does seem like a very smart young lady."

Although still creasing his brow in confusion, the middle-aged man was now *praising* Alisa. Masachika, who was still smiling gently with a cold light in his eyes, lowered his tone and added:

"Right? She has her mother's hair, too. Her mother is not from Japan, by the way. What do you think? It's beautiful, isn't it?"

"Y-yeah…"

After taking a closer look at Alisa, the man probably realized Masachika must have been telling the truth when he noticed her "non-Japanese" features. Awkwardly, he then faced Alisa and slightly lowered his head as if he had suddenly sobered up even more.

"I, uh… I apologize for my rude behavior. Being intoxicated is not an excuse."

Masachika dropped the piercing glare and calmly replied:

"We accept your apology. Right?"

"…"

He glanced back at Alisa over his shoulder, but her eyes were silently still locked on the man. Nevertheless, Masachika nodded as if things were settled, wrapped an arm around Alisa to hide her expression, and encouraged Alisa to walk away with him.

"Well, we should be going."

And just like that, he led Alisa away. After they walked in silence for the next few minutes until the businessmen could no longer be seen, Masachika took his hand off her shoulder and sighed.

"Seriously, Alya? What you did was dangerous. He was drunk. You knew you were going to piss him off, didn't you?"

"...I don't care if he was drunk or not. I couldn't let him insult my parents like that."

"What you did was still reckless, though. What if he punched you?"

"I may not look like it, but I'm trained in self-defense. I can handle a drunk," replied Alisa in a flat voice as if she was forcing her overflowing anger back down her throat. Masachika understood where she was coming from, which was why he had no idea how he should handle this.

"At any rate, he admitted he was wrong. Let's just let it go."

"...Fine."

After Alisa let out a deep sigh, her expression returned to normal, and she regained her composure.

"By the way, you two knew each other?"

"No? I have no idea who he was."

"...What?"

Her jaw dropped. Masachika's lips curled into a half smile as he added:

"I surprised myself, really. I wasn't confident that I could lie to his face and get away with it."

"W-wait! What?! So, like, you seriously had never met him before today?! What about your brother's wedding?!"

"I don't even have a brother."

"Wh-what the...?"

"I get that he was drunk, but I still can't believe it went that well. My heart was racing the entire time. Ha-ha-ha! Ah, thank goodness that worked." Masachika laughed, acting innocent. Alisa, on the other hand, looked like she had a headache.

"...What was the point of all that?"

"Hmm? Uh... He was intoxicated, for starters. Plus, with all that blood rushing to his head, I figured I'd bring up work to try to calm him down. And..."

"And what?"

Masachika shrugged after glancing at Alisa and seeing her suspicious glare.

"...What he said really pissed me off, so I thought I'd threaten him a little. And hey, it worked. Nobody got into a fight, and he even ended up apologizing. Can't imagine a better outcome than that."

"*Sigh*... I'm impressed that you can tell one lie after the other like that on the spot. I think you have the potential to be a con artist."

"Rude. I am insulted you would say such a thing about a pure and innocent little boy like me."

"Uh-huh..."

"Oh, come on. Don't look at me with dead eyes like that. This is way worse than being insulted."

Alisa snorted out a laugh at the pathetic look on Masachika's face. She then promptly started walking ahead, but Masachika quickly caught up until he was by her side.

"Thanks," she muttered faintly while still looking ahead.

"No problem," he replied while still looking forward as well. They didn't say another word to each other after that. They continued on in silence until Alisa eventually stopped in front of her apartment complex.

"This your place?"

"Yes. Thank you for walking me home."

"No problem."

As they faced each other at the entrance, Masachika nervously scratched his head before giving her one last reminder.

"Hey, I know it's pretty unlikely something like this will ever happen again, but if it does and you're alone, ignore it. It's not worth the risk."

"What, are you worried about me?" Alisa smirked teasingly.

"Yeah, I'm worried about you. You can be socially inept at times," replied Masachika, looking her straight in the eye. She blinked a few times at the serious response, then softly muttered:

"Oh."

Alisa turned around and faced the entrance.

"...I guess I'll start being a little more careful, then."

"I appreciate it."

"..."

She walked a few steps forward before stopping in front of the automatic door.

"Hey, Kuze," she said without looking back.

"Yeah?"

"Are you really not interested in joining the student council?"

"Wait. Seriously? You too?"

"Just answer the question."

There was no way he would be able to joke his way out of answering that firm tone. His smirk faded.

"I'm not interested in joining the student council," he replied in a tone just as firm as hers to make it clear there was no hope of him ever joining.

"If..."

But she didn't back down. There was even a sense of urgency in her voice as she continued:

"If I..."

But it ended there, and a few seconds of silence followed.

"Forget it. Good night."

"Good night."

After making sure Alisa got inside her apartment complex safely, Masachika turned on his heel, looked up at the night sky, and muttered to himself:

"What do they expect from me? Both Alya and Yuki."

He had a rough idea what Alisa had wanted to say, and that was exactly why he pretended not to know.

"I can't do anything," he added in a self-deprecating manner before he set out for his own home, smothered in a faintly blue cloud of loneliness.

"I'm home."

When Masachika stepped inside his apartment, he noticed a pair of shoes lined up on the floor and raised an eyebrow. He and his father were the only ones who lived here, and his father was currently abroad for business as a diplomat. And yet there was a pair of shoes set neatly that wasn't his nor his father's.

The hell? I thought she said she was going home.

Masachika headed straight to the living room with a crease still in his brow, opened the door to said living room, and found Yuki there. She was dressed in a long-sleeved shirt and sweatpants, with her hair sloppily tied up in a ponytail, while sitting in a chair and watching anime on TV like she owned the place.

"Oh, hey. Did you get Alya home safely?"

"What are you doing here?"

"Huh? I'm staying here tonight."

"I didn't hear anything about you staying here tonight."

"Because I didn't tell you," Yuki stated calmly while still facing the TV. Both her appearance and behavior bore absolutely no similarities to the perfect young gentlewoman everyone knew and loved at school. It was such a dramatic change that people who had never seen her like this before would believe it was merely someone who resembled Yuki.

The anime came to an end, and a commercial began to play. It was for a dark-fantasy comic getting a live-action movie.

"I'm seeing this tomorrow," Yuki suddenly revealed, pointing at the screen.

"Cool."

"And you're comin' with me."

"First I'm hearing about this."

"Because I'm tellin' ya now for the first time."

Masachika glanced at the commercial while Yuki sighed, showing no signs of guilt.

"I thought you hated live-action adaptions like this."

"Stop! I don't want to hear it!" Yuki suddenly shouted, thrusting her palm forward as if to keep Masachika from making any more casual remarks. She then hastily sputtered, "I know, I know. Once they announced the cast, I figured there was a ninety percent chance it was going to suck! And to tell the truth, the commercials aren't doing it any favors, either! But I think it's wrong to just put it down without giving it a fair chance first. It might actually not be a train wreck. It could even turn out to be a hidden gem! I know. I get it. The only reason they keep producing these trash live-action adaptions is because people like me keep spending money to go see them. I know it's my fault!"

"Okay, okay, okay. Let's calm down and take a deep breath. I feel like you're about to tell me you know a dark secret you weren't supposed to know."

"Because I do! I know that we're not related by blood, Masachika! We may be brother and sister, but... Ahem! What are you trying to make me say?! We're *definitely* blood related."

"I like how you emphasized 'definitely.'"

"I mean, it does happen sometimes. You think you're siblings, but you're actually cousins. I guess that doesn't really count, since cousins are still blood related, but you get my point."

"Yeah, and being cousins is okay because you're not actually siblings."

"You're clueless."

"What are you talking about?"

"Ugh! Actually, being siblings is what makes it good!" Yuki insisted passionately with her eyes opened wide.

"Makes what good?!"

Yuki Suou. While she played Masachika's childhood friend at school, she was actually a fellow nerd and friend...as well as his biological sister, who went to live with their mother when their parents got divorced.

CHAPTER 6 — This is the first time I have ever seen the shadow of death.

A long time ago, when I was in elementary school, I was at a park near Grandpa's house, which I would always run straight to on my way home after school. I darted my eyes around at the entrance, and I saw her sitting on a plastic dome with a few tunnels going through it.

"<Hey, ——!>"

When I called out her name and rushed over, she looked at me with stars in her eyes and instantly cracked a smile as she waved.

"<Mashachika!>"

"<For the last time, my name is Ma-*sa*-chika!>"

I corrected her with a smirk like I always did, but she merrily laughed as if she didn't care. Seeing her smile like that made me not care anymore, either.

"<Masaaachika, come up here with me!>"

"<Seriously?>"

"<Come on! Hurry!>"

"<Fine.>"

The plastic dome had a ladder bolted into its side, so I placed my backpack on the ground and climbed on top of the dome with my tiny arms and legs, struggling all the way.

"<Ta-daa! I'm here!>"

She welcomed me with a smile as her long, golden hair glittered in the evening sun. I can still remember the look in her mirthfully creased blue eyes.

"<Look, look! The sunset is beautiful!>"

"<Yeah, it really is.>"

We sat and watched the sun set together while talking about nothing in particular. I technically did most of the talking, though.

"<And this Seiren Academy is actually the school that my parents went to. It's apparently really, really hard to get into, but they said it'd be a breeze for someone with grades like mine.>"

"<Wow, Masaaachika! You can do anything!>"

"<Heh. I wish.>"

She gave me genuine praise and even seemed like she enjoyed listening to my constant bragging. I felt so happy and proud whenever she complimented me. I would have done anything for her, no matter how difficult, whether it be studying, sports, or even music.

"<Ah, we should start heading home...>"

It was a rule between us that we'd say our good-byes once it got dark.

"<Good night, Masaaachika. See you tomorrow.>"

"<Yeah, see you tomorrow, ——.>"

She then gave me a big hug and a kiss on the cheek. I was too embarrassed to hug and kiss her back, but it honestly made me really happy. After letting me go, she affectionately smiled and—

"Wham!"

"Oof?!"

My upper body was suddenly crushed, forcing my brain to awaken.

"Cough! Hack! Hff!"

"GOOD MORNING, MY DEAR BROTHER!"

"Ngh... It was good until you showed up!"

After finally catching my breath, I glared up at Yuki, who was grinning down from on top of me, raising an eyebrow as if she was confused.

"Hmm? What are ya mad about? Pretty sure it's every high school boy's dream to get body-pressed by their cute little sister. You should be smiling, punk."

"Don't give me any of that *it was just a prank, bro* crap. Ever heard of DV?"

"Are you calling me your darling Venus?! Oh my gosh! You're such a *siscon*! ♡"

"*Domestic violence*! And I don't have a sister complex! You really had to do some mental gymnastics for that one, huh?!"

"Hmm... What exactly is bothering you this morning, Masachika?"

"Everything."

Yuki pouted while furrowing her brow, seemingly in thought, then suddenly snapped her fingers as if she had an epiphany.

"Now I get it! You didn't want me to wake you up with a body press. You wanted me to slip under the covers with you so you could wake up to me by your side."

"It would actually be pretty terrifying if you did something like that for real."

"Wait. Does that mean...you'd rather me hide under the bed? You're such a freak."

"That'd be *extremely* terrifying!"

"Fine... I'll hide under the bed next time so the moment you step out of bed, I can grab your ankles."

"Are you trying to kill me?"

"A little sister who scares her brother awake every morning... It's a pretty original concept. Don't you think?"

"It's a little too original for my taste... Now get off me."

Yuki, who was still on top of me while kicking her legs up and down, smirked and curiously tilted her head.

"Why? Is this making you feel something?"

"Go kill yourself."

I sent my sister a piercing subzero gaze at point-blank range for soiling my ears with such filth this early in the morning, causing her to cackle as she got off me and left the room.

"*Sigh...*"

I was finally able to sit up in my own bed.

"..."

I'd had a dream that took me way back. It was a memory of my first love. It was a memory of the most brilliant period of my life. I met her at that park. We used to play all the time. I even started seriously learning Russian because I wanted to talk to her so badly. Even though my parents were always fighting and I was staying at my grandfather's place, I wasn't lonely because she was there for me. Yeah... I'd been in love with her. And yet...I still couldn't remember her name or what she looked like.

"...Tsk."

I really was my mother's son. I was a heartless person. I so easily forgot someone I once claimed to love so much. Something cold began to fill my chest. The burning love and motivation I felt back then was now buried so far down that it wasn't even visible anymore. There was a reason I lost all my motivation to do anything. There was someone I could blame. But no matter the excuse or who I blamed, the truth of the matter was that I was simply a lazy sack of garbage. I romanticized notions of hard work yet loathed it. I was the kind of human filth who was satisfied knowing that he was trash, since some never figured it out. That's the kind of person I was.

"And someone like that isn't fit for the student council..."

Let alone being the vice president. And I already knew it wouldn't work because I had half-heartedly taken Yuki up on her offer to become the vice president of the student council in middle school. A position like that was not something anyone should do without passion and resolution. When Yuki was elected president, I saw the other candidate weeping behind the auditorium. Her eyes were swollen. She was sobbing to her friends that she had let her parents down, and she had no idea how she was going to face them when she got home. We worked together in the student council during our first year of middle school and really got to know each other, so when I saw her like that, I was overcome with an incredible sense of guilt and shock. This was how she really felt, despite acting courageous in front of the others and wishing Yuki good luck earlier.

Yuki was no different. Her parents expected a lot from her. But me? The guy who only became the vice president because of his love for his sister and a sense of obligation? Did I have any right to kick that girl down like this? For the following year, I worked my ass off so I could overcome that guilt, but it never went away. I never want to feel that way aga—

"*Wham!* Whaddaya think you're doin', goin' back to sleep?! ...Oh, you're awake?"

"Can you stop kicking my door open like that? You've already put a dent in it after kicking it so many times."

I knew I was wasting my breath, but there *was* a small dent in my door slightly under the doorknob, which was strangely smoother than the surrounding wood. Yuki glanced at the dent, then smiled with evident satisfaction for some bizarre reason.

"I bet I can turn it into a hole with a few more years."

"Stop training for karate matches using my door."

"There are countless heroines who have kicked doors off the hinges around the world, but I'm going to be the first who slowly drills a hole through one over the years."

"I'm pretty sure there really aren't that many women who have kicked doors off their hinges."

It wasn't like Yuki was actually kicking the door wide-open, either; she always turned the doorknob a little first. Why she did this was a mystery.

"Anyway, hurry up and get out of bed. Your adorable little sister made you breakfast."

"Yeah, yeah."

When I walked into the living room, I actually was welcomed with breakfast, but...

"What is it, my dear brother?"

"...What's this?"

I pointed at the semisolid, mushy egg dish on the plate in the very middle, which was in layers here and there. Yuki blinked a few times, then innocently replied:

"Huh? Those are scrambled eggs."

"Just admit you were trying to make a Japanese omelet, and then this happened."

"…I have no clue what you're talking about."

I buried my reproachful gaze in the back of her head as she looked away, making it obvious I was right. To be honest, though, it actually wasn't that bad. Once you added a little ketchup, it had a sort of East meets West taste to it…

After watching the movie as planned, Masachika and Yuki headed toward the exit along with the crowd and left the theater, which was on the top floor of a large commercial complex, then got on the escalator.

"Ngh…!"

Yuki stretched her arms and back.

"That was trash!" she declared with a sigh of relief.

"Could you be any blunter?"

"It was even worse than I thought it'd be. You really can't put these cutesy idols in dark-fantasy worlds and expect it to work. It just looked like she was cosplaying the entire movie. It didn't help that they spent the whole budget on the fight scenes and didn't put effort into anything else. There's no way you could keep up if you didn't read the comics."

"Yeah. But at least the action scenes were pretty cool," replied Masachika with a bitter smile as Yuki continued to diss the movie while cheerfully smiling. It was still a little early for lunch, so they continued to walk around the shopping center while discussing the film.

"Oh, look at this outfit. It's so cute. I've been wanting a new summer dress, but I planned on splurging at the anime store after this…"

"Fifteen thousand yen?! Seriously?!"

"You should try to dress nicer, too, sometimes. It's not like you don't have any money."

"Yeah, I don't get anywhere near as much allowance as you."

"Sure, but you don't spend all your money buying nerdy things like me."

Yuki had a point. Unlike her, Masachika wasn't a collector of anime goods. He hardly spent money on comics or light novels, either. Then again, he didn't really have to, because Yuki hid all her nerd gear at Masachika's house so she could keep her hobby a secret. Therefore, he could borrow and read whatever light novel or comic he was interested in, instead of having to buy them himself. In fact, Yuki was even the one who converted him into a nerd.

"You wore those clothes last year. It's time you buy something new."

"Says the girl wearing my old clothes."

Yuki was wearing a somewhat baggy, long-sleeved undershirt and jeans like a tomboy, but those clothes were actually Masachika's hand-me-downs.

"Yeah, but I look good in this. Jeans get better with age."

"Uh-huh… By the way, my dear sister…"

"Yes, my brother?"

"Is it just my imagination, or do you also notice something silver flickering out of the corner of your eye?"

"I don't think it's just your imagination, Brother."

"That's what I thought. I should have guessed when you let your hair down. You're in gentlewoman mode, to boot."

Yuki had undone her ponytail, and while she spoke in her natural speaking voice, her behavior was very elegant, as if she were at school.

"Heh! I noticed a long time ago, Brother."

"Seriously? When?"

"Almost immediately after getting off the escalator."

"That long ago? I'm impressed."

"Heh… I have a supernatural sense that allows me to immediately detect the gazes of people I know."

"Wow. I'm surprised…that you're not even embarrassed for saying that."

"Heh... I'm extremely embarrassed."

"Then wipe that smug grin off your face."

The siblings could still feel someone staring hard at them from behind even as they did their bit. The clear reflection of an all-too-familiar silver-haired girl could be seen in a shop's window as she tried to hide behind a column. And perhaps this was Masachika's imagination, but he could practically see a dark thundercloud hanging over her head.

What should I do?

Would it be best to talk to her? Or wait for her to come over and say something? Or maybe running away would be the best option? As Masachika considered all his options...

"Oh my. Alya?" Yuki said casually as if she had just noticed Alisa after slowly turning around.

Yukiiiiiiiii!!

Masachika inwardly screamed at her sudden, reckless decision to strike head-on, but they were at the point of no return now. After mustering up the courage, he put on a look of surprise and turned around as well.

"Oh, wow. It is Alya. What a coincidence."

Even Masachika himself wasn't really confident in his acting, but Alisa apparently had too much on her mind to even notice. She messed around with the smartphone in her hands, then approached them, her eyes wandering left and right.

"Yes, what a coincidence. I, uh... I saw you two together a few minutes ago, but I didn't want to interrupt your conversation...," mumbled Alisa as if she was still somewhat flustered.

That was way more than a few minutes.

The siblings thought the exact same thing at the exact same moment, but they didn't show any indication of that on their face. Masachika couldn't help but give Yuki a lukewarm glare, but she was already in her proper-young-lady mode.

"Oh, okay," she innocently replied. "Anyway, what brings you here?"

"I'm shopping for new clothes…"

"Oh, really? Have you already had lunch?"

"Not yet."

"Then how about we have lunch together? It's—"

"Hold on," interrupted Masachika. He then grimaced at Yuki's composed expression and asked:

"Don't tell me you plan on taking Alya to *that* restaurant?"

"Why not? You were really looking forward to it."

"We should go somewhere else if Alya's going to be eating with us."

"Why? Is there some sort of problem?" inquired Alisa as they seemed to ignore her while arguing over who knows what.

"Alya, do you hate spicy food?"

"Spicy food? I mean, I don't really hate it…"

"The restaurant we were actually planning on going to is famous for spicy ramen, but if you're fine with spicy food, then—"

"Stop downplaying it. Alya, I'm gonna be straight with you. *Spicy* is an understatement. It's a restaurant that specializes in burning-hot ramen. I've never been, either, but it's probably not something you can enjoy if you don't like extremely spicy food. So—"

"Let's go," Alisa interjected, cutting Masachika off. Seeing her expression alone was enough to know it was hopeless to convince her otherwise, and he fell silent for a few moments.

"I really don't think this is a good idea. There are plenty of other restaurants around here…"

"But you were really looking forward to it, right? So let's go. Besides, I'd feel guilty if you changed your plans because of me."

"You don't have to come, you know?"

"Oh? Is there a problem if I tag along?"

"That's not what I meant, but I don't remember seeing you ever eat spicy food…"

"I don't dislike spicy food."

Masachika was skeptical, but he couldn't just flat out call her a liar. That said, he had a feeling she was more into sweets than spicy food. He had never asked her directly about it, but after all the time he'd spent with her, he had a good idea of what she liked. Spicy food, though? He had no idea. He had never seen her eat anything spicy, and that was the only information he had to go by.

Well, she says she wants to go, and they probably have some not-so-spicy food on the menu as well, so...

With that mindset, Masachika decided to head to the restaurant, albeit with a bit of anxiety.

◇

"...Is this the place?"

"Yep."

Outside the shopping center, they walked a short while down a narrow path until they arrived at a ramen shop. Alisa looked up at the sign and grimaced.

I don't blame her.

But while Masachika understood her reaction, Yuki was full of smiles.

"The sign says, *The Cauldron of Hell.* Are you sure they serve ramen here?"

"Of course I'm sure."

"But it says *Hell* on the sign..."

"Don't worry, Alya. This is the place. Here, it says the name of the restaurant on the menu, too."

"...Oh."

Although it still didn't make her feel any better, Alisa nodded with a grimace, as if she was paralyzed due to shock.

"You sure you don't want to go somewhere else?"

But Masachika's thoughtfulness suddenly triggered Alisa's determination, and he was met with a piercing glare.

"Don't be ridiculous. I was only a little surprised by how unique this place turned out to be."

"Uh-huh..."

He knew there was nothing he could say to convince her once her utter hatred for defeat crept out, so he gave up and followed Yuki into the restaurant.

"Welcome!"

They were immediately welcomed by a man's well-projected voice as the pungent scent of spicy food irritated their noses.

"Gmph?!"

Masachika suddenly heard a faint gag coming from behind.

"How many in your group?"

"Three."

"All right. This way, please."

The waiter walked them over to three seats at the counter. When Masachika glanced over at Alisa to his right, she was holding her nose, with tears welling in her eyes. While Masachika and Yuki were used to the smell due to constantly eating out at spicy restaurants, Alisa seemed to be in pain.

"Are you okay?"

"Why wouldn't I be?" replied Alisa in a hushed voice, making it clear that she was just acting tough. She then tightly shut her eyes, did away with the tears, and tried to pretend like nothing was wrong as she reached for the menu…but the moment she opened it, she froze.

"…Hey."

"Hmm?"

"I have no idea what I'm even looking at."

"Yeah…" Masachika awkwardly nodded. It made sense because with violent names like *Blood Pond Hell* and *Spike Pit Hell*, it was hard to imagine this was even food. Yuki, her hair tied in a low ponytail, then began explaining the menu as if she were a regular.

"The Blood Pond Hell is a ramen known for its bloodred soup base, just as the name suggests, and is the mildest ramen on the menu. Spike Pit Hell, on the other hand, is a spicier dish that makes it feel like your tongue is being pierced by a thousand needles, as the name suggests."

"O-oh… Well, then…"

Alisa meekly lowered her gaze toward the very bottom of the menu as she grimaced.

"What about the *Hell of Uninterrupted Suffering*?" Alisa asked timidly. Yuki immediately smiled proudly, as if she had been waiting for the question.

"It's apparently so spicy that you lose all feeling!"

"Are you sure that's not nerve damage?"

Alisa's expression fell with despair, as if she had finally realized how terrifying this restaurant really was. Masachika, by her side, also looked over the menu one more time, only to realize that even the least hot ramen was still really hot. He closed his eyes.

"I guess I'll go with the Blood Pond Hell, since the common rule is to go for the standard dish when it's your first time."

"Y-yeah, the basics are important, after all."

"Oh? You two are going to order the same thing? I guess I'll order that as well, then."

Masachika offered what help he could, which Alisa thankfully accepted, and was followed by Yuki. Thus, they all ended up ordering the same thing.

"At any rate, I was kind of surprised to see you dressed somewhat boyish today, Yuki."

"*Giggle.* I thought I'd switch things up a little, since it's the weekend."

"Really? Well, you almost look like a completely different person. You still look really good, though."

"Thank you. You look really good today yourself. It's not often I see you in something other than your school uniform. I thought you were a professional model for a second there."

"Really? Thanks."

Masachika felt both uncomfortable and happy to be in between two girls chatting it up, but he began to break into a cold sweat as the surrounding men glared at him. The look the ~ ' waiter, who seemed to be around the same age as him, was giving him was the worst. They were the eyes a man would use only on his worst enemy, but Masa-chika really was surrounded by two beautiful women, so he couldn't complain. Not only were they beautiful, but they were also essentially without equal, so it was simply normal for an average-looking guy like Masachika to be stared at. It was also perfectly natural for a nerd to get excited and think, *Wait. Am I the protagonist of a rom-com?! Is this my harem?!*

They aren't fighting over me, though. Plus, I probably just look like their professional bag carrier from the viewpoint of an onlooker.

And it was just how Masachika imagined it. Everyone's curious stares faded once they realized the girls were ignoring him and chat-ting with each other. Even the waiter, who was glaring at him with envy and hatred, softened his gaze and went back to work…and that was when Yuki decided to drop a bomb.

"This shirt and these jeans actually used to be Masachika's."

Alisa's smile froze, and the temperature in the restaurant plummeted.

Yukiiiiiiiii!!

The curious looks in the restaurant began to refocus on him. Even the waiter was looking back and forth between Yuki and Masachika as if he couldn't believe what he was seeing.

"He gave you those?"

"Yes, my family wants me to dress 'ladylike'…but I've always wanted to dress more boyish like this, so I asked Masachika for some of his old clothes."

"Oh…"

Alisa's smirk turned into an ominous faint smile as she hit Masa-chika with a penetrating glare.

"I didn't realize being childhood friends made two people so close. I didn't know Kuze liked dressing girls up in his old clothes, either. Interesting hobby."

"It's not a hobby."

"Yes, it isn't his hobby. It's his fetish."

"You shut up."

He glared at Yuki as if to tell her to not say another word, but she simply seemed confused.

"Hmm? But I clearly remember you being thrilled when you first saw me wearing a boyfriend shirt."

"That never happened!"

Yuki continued to drop bomb after bomb without even a hint of guilt, creating a stir in the restaurant. Listeners took "That never happened!" to mean that he hadn't been "thrilled" when she wore the shirt. Yuki did, however, wear his old shirts from time to time. She would visit his house on a whim without a change of clothes sometimes, so she would wear his old clothes as pajamas. However, she was the one who had jumped up and down in excitement when she first put on his old clothes while shouting, *"Boyfriend shirt, boyfriend shirt!"* Masachika, on the other hand, simply rolled his eyes, but no one would ever know the truth except for them.

"...What's a boyfriend shirt?"

Thankfully Alisa didn't know what a "boyfriend shirt" was, since she wasn't into geek culture. Yuki leaned toward her with the smile of an angel and the whisper of a devil to ask if she wanted to know what it was, but Masachika promptly began to interrupt her. However, before he could even do that, the waiter came over with their ramen, glaring at Masachika as if Masachika had killed his parents.

"Sorry to keep you waiting. Three orders of Blood Pond Hell."

One glance down at the ramen before her sent Alisa rearing back with a grunt as she choked a bit. The eye-burning steam apparently didn't do the dark-red soup, which was living up to its name, any favors. The spicy food–loving siblings, on the other hand, smiled and grabbed their chopsticks.

"We should hurry before the noodles get soggy."

"Good idea."

"Y-yeah..."

Masachika and Yuki dug into their noodles without a moment's hesitation while Alisa timidly slurped up her first bite.

"Mmmm! This is delicious!"

"Yeah, it really lives up to its reputation."

The siblings smiled with clear satisfaction after their first bite, but when Masachika glanced at Alisa…

"…"

…her entire body was tense, and her eyes were opened wide as she continued to chew without even blinking. Her left hand on the table was clenched ridiculously tight and trembled.

"You okay, Alya?"

"…! Yeah, it's…delicious."

Only after she swallowed the food in her mouth was she finally able to blink again and put on a calmer expression. Masachika felt both annoyance and admiration when he saw her still trying to act tough, and he handed her a napkin.

"You should wipe your lips after every bite, or your lips are going to swell."

"…Thanks."

Masachika went straight back to his ramen after making sure she wiped her lips, and the powerful punch from the cayenne pepper filled his mouth after every slurp. It was so hot that he began to sweat, but the spiciness really brought out the other ingredients' flavors, making him crave even more. He wanted to peek into the abyss of the red sea. (This is Masachika's personal opinion alone and should be regarded as such.)

"Man, this is good." Masachika exhaled in satisfaction. But all of a sudden, he heard a whisper tickle his ear.

"<It hurtsss.>"

It was a pitiful cry coming from the young woman at his side. When he glanced over, he noticed Alisa's chopsticks were frozen in place. While she was maintaining her composure, she apparently couldn't move her chopsticks another inch. That was when she realized Masachika was looking at her, so she shoved her chopsticks into the bowl as if she had no other choice.

"No, wait. Alya, you don't have to force yourself to eat that."

"I'm not. I already told you it's delicious."

And yet you said it hurts in Russian just a second ago.

"But… Yeah, okay. If you say so."

Masachika wondered if she'd be all right, but he knew he had to give up because nothing he was going to say would stop her. After drinking some water and taking a short break, Alisa brought her chopsticks toward the ramen once more when…

"<I can't take it anymore…>"

I can't concentrate like this!

The voice coming from his side was so feeble that it made him feel pity; he tried not to care as he continued his meal when all of a sudden—

"<Mommy…>"

Once Alisa started clinging on to her imaginary mother, Masachika looked at her, unable to stand idly by.

Yeah, this isn't going to work. Her pupils are dilated.

Surprisingly, Alisa's expression still hadn't changed at all…but the shadow of death was on her face. It was hopeless. Masachika was planning on letting her have her fun until she gave up on her own, but it was getting dangerous. The doctor had to get into the ring and stop the fight.

"Al—"

Right as Masachika tried to stop her, Yuki spoke up as if to get the first word out and cut him off.

"How is it, Alya?"

Alisa's wandering eyes suddenly focused at the sound of her future campaign rival's voice. Her fighting spirit was summoned, bringing life back into her body as she even managed to smile.

"It's delicious."

"Oh, that's wonderful. I am so happy to hear that you love spicy food, too."

Yuki innocently smiled back at Alisa's somewhat ghastly, fierce smirk. She then held out a condiment to Alisa while still innocently smiling.

"This restaurant has something called Demon Tears, which can make the food even spicier. Would you like to try it?"

Yuki was basically attacking a fleeing enemy. The corner of Alisa's lips twitched. By the way, Demon Tears were a type of seasoning, and its official name was *Even the Evilest of Demons Get Tears in Their Eyes*. It was an original blend created by this restaurant.

Stop torturing her! Alya doesn't even have any HP left!

Masachika was inwardly shouting when he came to a startling realization.

Oh! There was no way for Yuki to have noticed, since Alya was complaining in Russian.

Once he realized that oversight, he leaned in to whisper into Yuki's ear...when he realized something else. While Yuki might have appeared to be smiling innocently, there was a sadistic fire burning in the depths of her eyes.

She's doing this on purpose?!

As Masachika shuddered, a pale-white hand reached for the condiment.

"All you need are a few drops for it to taste amazing."

"Wait! Alya?! I really don't recommend doing that!"

But his warnings were in vain, for Alisa took the lid off the container, grabbed the tiny spoon, and scooped some of the dark-red liquid, which she then sprinkled into her ramen. And a few seconds later...

"...?!?!"

The restaurant was filled with Alisa's voiceless screams.

CHAPTER 7

That was quite the tragedy, wasn't it?

"Are you okay, Alya?"

"…"

Masachika timidly called out to Alisa as she limply sank onto a bench in the park near the ramen shop, but she didn't reply. She didn't even have the energy to pretend like she was okay anymore as she slowly passed into the next world. She sat with her elbows on her knees and her forehead resting in both hands in silence, as if she were a philosopher deep in thought. Masachika scratched his head, pondering what he could do, but before he could figure anything out, she gradually lifted her head and sluggishly searched the park with her vacant eyes.

"…Where's Yuki?"

"Oh, she said she had to pick up something at the store, so she left. She'll meet up with us when she's done."

"…Oh."

And by "store," he meant the anime store. She decided to go empty out her wallet while Alisa was in a daze. Even though they were friends in the student council, Yuki seemed to want to keep her nerdy hobbies a secret.

"Are you okay?"

"Why wouldn't I be?"

"What? Uh…"

It seemed Alisa still didn't want to admit defeat, despite not being able to stand. She technically didn't lose, since she stubbornly forced herself to eat every last bite, but…but that begged the question: What was she even fighting against?

"So, uh…want some ice cream?" asked Masachika after darting his eyes around the park and spotting an ice-cream truck.

"…Yes."

Alisa was unusually honest about what she wanted for a change, so they got some ice cream and returned to their bench when…

"…"

Masachika licked his chocolate chip ice cream while staring hard at the ice cream in Alisa's hand. Unlike Masachika, who went for the cone, she went for the cup and decided on chocolate, vanilla, cheesecake, and cookies-and-cream ice cream—all the sweetest flavors. "Green tea? Chocolate mint? Ice cream wasn't supposed to be bitter or refreshing! Cones were a waste of stomach room, too!" That was what her bold choices said for her. Even the guy making her ice cream was a little surprised.

"…It's only because I just ate something spicy," argued Alisa, bashfully looking away from him as if she'd noticed his half-surprised, half-amazed stare.

"Okay."

It was still overly sweet and excessive, thought Masachika. For some reason, Alisa was hiding her love of sweets. Maybe she felt that it didn't fit her image.

The fact that she drinks red-bean soup like water and claims her brain needs the sugar and she needs the energy makes it kind of pointless to hide it, though.

Nevertheless, Masachika never attempted to call her out, since she clearly wanted to keep it a secret. He believed that no matter how obvious it might be, you should respect others trying to be the person they wanted to be.

Could she have had a more difficult personality?

How stubborn and vain could one person be? Alisa had worked on herself over the years to become her ideal self, and Masachika respected that. Watching her work so hard even brought a smile to his face, which was why he naturally wanted to help her. He wanted to make sure her hard work paid off. Whether that was some overwhelming desire to protect others or merely something he did to make amends for his father's and his past was a mystery to even Masachika himself.

It's a crappy reason to do something, regardless.

But while he was mocking his reasoning, he suddenly found himself curious about something else.

"Hey, Alya."

"Yes?"

"Why do you want to be the president of the student council?"

"Because I do. I'm aiming for the top. Do I need any more of a reason than that?"

It would be hard to explain that her extremely bare response was a satisfying answer to his question, but Masachika realized that was how she actually felt. Perhaps Alisa herself didn't know exactly why she wanted to do it. She simply had to run, no matter what. Whenever she found a mountain, she had to climb it. That was just who Alisa Mikhailovna Kujou was.

I'm jealous. She's incredible.

And he genuinely felt that way. He was impressed by the beauty of someone pursuing their ideals and continuously working hard toward their goals. There was something noble about people who continued to push forward on their own two feet without relying on others.

Only people who took pride in what they did and fully committed themselves to their lives had souls that gave off a brilliant glow, and Masachika could clearly see that in Alisa. Yuki and Touya had that same glow, but what Alisa had was even brighter yet also somehow uncertain.

"If you're going to run for president, then does that mean you have a vice president already lined up to run with you?"

After Alisa's eyes briefly wavered, she faced Masachika with a bold expression, as if she was embarrassed for getting flustered.

"I don't, but that isn't going to be a problem because I don't need a vice president."

"Uh… You have to run together as a team. That's the rule."

"I only need a vice president in name only. I'm sure I'll be able to find someone who'd like the title."

Masachika was suddenly overcome with loneliness. This was it. This was why Alisa's glow looked so uncertain. She didn't consider going to others for help, and she didn't expect anything from others. She wasn't interested in acceptance or praise. What drove Alisa for results were her ideals and her ideals alone…or perhaps it was for her own satisfaction, which was why she believed she couldn't rely on others. Be that as it may, Masachika couldn't just leave her like this, because he knew there was only so much one person could do, and he knew how depressing, painful, and empty it felt when hard work didn't pay off.

Hard work should be rewarded. People who actually put in the effort deserve their desired results.

Those beliefs were part of why he always wanted to help Alisa. He would get those around her more involved so she would have no choice but to work together with them, and he took the initiative to call her by her nickname. Why? Because he wanted to make her more approachable. Though, it didn't seem to be working that well by the look of things.

"…Huh."

"…"

Alisa didn't say another word, nor did she show anything that would resemble an emotion. As she silently ate her ice cream, Masachika felt as if her silence was a plea, but perhaps that was merely his ego making him believe that. What was it that Alisa was going to tell him the previous day before she stepped into her apartment? But she confirmed his suspicions right after she finished eating her ice cream.

"<If we were together…>"

However, she fell silent before finishing her sentence, as if she was afraid of what he might think, despite the fact that she was speaking in Russian. But for Masachika, that was more than enough.

But I...

He didn't have the glow that Alisa, Yuki, and Touya possessed. He didn't have the passion to continuously work hard toward a certain goal that he himself had come up with. He always let others decide the goal for him, and how passionate he was depended on the other person. He'd always been this way, even during the period of his life in which he shined the most.

His mother and his grandfather had given him the goal to become someone worthy of taking over the Suou household, but his enthusiasm toward this goal depended only on his mother and *that girl.* Masachika wasn't passionate about the idea itself. He only worked hard because he desired his mother's praise along with the praise of that young girl. All he did was run on the fuel given to him on the path laid out for him. But now that they were both gone, he couldn't go anywhere. He was stuck in place.

I'm not good enough.

Masachika was grateful that she had said that in Russian, because if it had been in Japanese, he would have probably chosen cowardly silence as his reply.

"Kuze, do you have any other plans today?"

"Hmm? Oh, not really."

"What about Yuki?"

"Oh... She'll probably call whenever she's done."

"Then help me finish my shopping."

"Didn't you say you were shopping for new clothes?"

"Yes. And...?"

"It's just... I thought there had to be a certain amount of intimacy between a guy and a girl before he got to help her pick out her new clothes."

"Really?"

Masachika's eyes opened wide in surprise when he saw the puzzled look on Alisa's face.

Ohhh... Alisa's never had any friends she can go shopping with, so it's hard for her to pick up on subtle things like this... Sniffle!

The pity he felt caused the inner corners of his eyes to burn as he tightly clenched his teeth, but his expression was brimming with compassion.

"Yeah…I'll help you. Let's go."

Alisa knit her brow at how understanding he'd suddenly become.

"Why the sudden change of heart?"

"Uh… Because we're friends, of course. Yep."

"I find it hard to believe that's why."

"Don't worry about it," joked Masachika, evading her question. After that, they returned to the shopping center they met at before lunch, went to the floor with all the clothing shops, and began their exploration. But the entire time, Alisa couldn't help but wonder why he was acting so nice all of a sudden, and her curiosity slowly transformed into misunderstanding.

Wait… Does he think I'm going to lose the race for student council president? Is that why he's being nice all of a sudden? Tsk! How dare he look down on me like this?!

She was mentally clenching her teeth because Masachika was treating her like a parent trying to cheer up his child. The way he was always seemed to think he was above others had always bothered her, but arguing with him and trying to rebel was something only a child would do.

I…I can't just let him treat me like this. I have to get back at him! I'm going to knock that smug look right off his face!

Alisa groaned to herself as she racked her brain…when she suddenly remembered what happened one morning the other day.

I'm going to put on the best fashion show he has ever seen until he starts getting hot and bothered!

There was a clothing store Alisa had been wanting to check out, and the moment she stepped inside, her outlandish decision, which had been born from an absurd misunderstanding, sent her straight to the changing room with a handful of various styles of clothing.

"I want to hear your opinion after I finish changing, okay?"

"Sure thing."

After closing the curtain between her and Masachika, she quickly began to examine the clothing.

I suppose I'll go with this one first...

The first article of clothing Alisa immediately reached for out of the bunch was a summery pure-white dress.

There's no way this isn't going to work! Masha even told me that all guys loved dresses like this!

Contrary to her competitive determination, Alisa decided to play it safe, perhaps unaware of her own competitive streak. She trusted the possibly unreliable information from her sister, who learned everything she knew from comic books. But when it was time to finally put on the dress and she reached for the button on her blouse, her hand froze.

Hold on... He can't hear me getting undressed, right?

There was only a thin piece of cloth separating her and Masachika. To make matters worse, the curtain didn't go all the way to the floor, so there was a slight gap. Alisa was suddenly overcome with embarrassment.

"Kuze! Stand a little farther away!" shouted Alisa from the other side of the curtain, unable to take it any longer.

"All right," lazily replied the voice, and the sound of footsteps slowly retreated into the distance. While she was somewhat relieved, she also began to panic because she could hear the footsteps far more clearly than she imagined she would.

Hmm? If I can hear his footsteps from here...does that mean he really can hear me undressing, too?

Alisa was no longer able to relax after realizing that she was doing something so embarrassing, and she felt that she finally understood what Masachika meant when he said he thought there had to be a certain amount of intimacy between a guy and a girl before he got to help her pick out her new clothes.

No, it's okay. There's music playing in the store, so he's probably not even going to be able to hear me at all...I hope.

Alisa was so embarrassed that she wanted to run away, but her pride wouldn't allow that. She swallowed her shame and finally began undressing. After she got changed as quickly and quietly as possible without thinking about the boy on the other side of the curtain, she strained her ears to see if she could hear Masachika, all while knowing it was pointless.

It looks like I'm okay...

She was satisfied when he didn't react, so she turned around and faced the mirror once more. Masachika, on the other hand, was busy trying to remain expressionless while the older women around him glanced warmly in his direction. "Oh my. Do you think he's waiting for his girlfriend? To be in high school and in love again... How cute," they said with their eyes.

This is just like a rom-com, thought Masachika as he tried to escape reality. Listening to her change didn't even cross his mind, nor did he even notice. Alisa's worries were all in her head. She would probably be pretty disappointed if she ever found out he was more concerned about the other women glancing at him than her getting changed, though.

Heh. Nice. I look really good, if I do say so myself.

She posed in front of the mirror while singing her own praises. She was sure of her victory (it was anyone's guess as to when this had become a contest) and began to reach for the curtain when she was suddenly struck with anxiety. What if he didn't react? What if he just said "Yeah, you look nice" while not paying attention and looking at his phone? ...It might make her cry. The thought alone was causing Alisa's heart to beat like a drum.

H-hmph! I'd slap the hell out of him if he did that!

Alisa swiftly flung open the curtain after pumping herself up and wrestling her anxiety to the ground.

"What do you think?"

She leaned into one leg with a hand on her hip, as if she was posing like a model, as she shot an instigating look at Masachika. She genuinely looked incredible thanks to her amazing body and good looks. Immediately, all the women throughout the store directed their gazes at her and gasped in admiration. Masachika was no exception.

Who doesn't *love it when girls dress like this?!*

Masachika powerfully shouted that in his heart while he slammed his fist onto an imaginary table. It looked like Ask Masha was right for a change. Nevertheless, Masachika knew that Alisa wanted him to drool over her. Whoever blushed first, lost. That was why he decided to not even attempt to evade but attack instead!

"You look incredible. The pure-white dress looks especially good on you, since you have such nice milky-white skin. It seriously emphasizes your clean, feminine look. I didn't think you could get any cuter, but here we are."

"…?! O-oh… Really…?"

Masachika's counterattack staggered her, and she started to feel jittery after being complimented in such a straightforward manner.

"Okay, let's try the next outfit…," muttered Alisa unintelligibly as she closed the curtain as if to run away, and they simultaneously crouched in a fluster the instant they could no longer see each other.

Wait, wait, wait, thought Alisa. *Hold on. What? He just showered me with compliments!*

Oh god! I'm so embarrassed! I can't believe I said all that without laughing! Masachika was reeling. *Holy crap. Saying that right to her face was so embarrassing! How is she always able to say stuff like that with a straight face?! I mean, she's doing it in Russian and thinks I don't understand, so I guess that makes sense, but still!*

Masachika clutched his head, fighting through the embarrassment with so much focus that he didn't have the energy to care about the surrounding women's heartwarming stares. Little did he know that Alisa was covering her cheeks while fighting through her embarrassment as well.

Wait. C-cute? D-do I look that cute? Wait, wait, wait! M-me? Did he say I was cute? Ahhh!

But she couldn't deal with the embarrassment and smacked the floor a few times…until she realized the noise she was making and stopped in a panic. After needlessly clearing her throat, she faced forward and gazed into the mirror…but when she noticed she was grinning from ear to ear, she instinctively bumped her forehead lightly against it. She rubbed her forehead against it, using the pain and chilling sensation to pull herself together.

Phew… I'm okay. Now that I think about it, he wasn't saying anything out of character. Of course he'd say something like that. Kuze's the kind of person who would compliment a girl. Very commendable of him, if I might add.

But when she threw her hair back while arrogantly judging him for some strange reason, she suddenly got the impression that he seemed very skilled.

Skilled at what, though?

But she didn't even have to think about it for more than a second. Masachika seemed like he was used to complimenting girls. But who had he been complimenting so much that made him get used to it? There was only one person who came to mind.

Yuki…?

The thought immediately cleared her head. She thought back to how they were having the time of their lives window-shopping together a few hours ago, and uneasiness spread through her heart.

"…"

After pulling herself away from the mirror, she looked down at the clothes and picked out a pair of jeans and a black T-shirt with some English written on it before changing once more. Perhaps Alisa had an idea why she went with a boyish outfit deep down inside but chose not to acknowledge it. If she said she selected the clothes for no particular reason, then that was that.

"So? How do I look?"

Alisa opened the curtain with an expression brimming with confidence as if to say, "I have nothing to hide." But Masachika wasn't so dense that he couldn't notice why she may have chosen such an outfit. He had enough tact (or perhaps brains) to not voice this out loud, though.

"You look really stylish in this outfit. You're more beautiful than cute if that makes any sense, so that outfit really looks good on you, too. Jeans seriously emphasize how nice your body is, unlike skirts."

"O-oh? I'll keep that in mind. Thanks."

Alisa accepted the excessive compliments this time without allowing herself to get flustered and thanked him with a smile, unusually enough.

"Let's move on to the next outfit, then."

"All right."

It wasn't long before Alisa had long forgotten her goal to make Masachika feel hot and bothered as she started to genuinely grow fond of the fashion show for what it was. She switched outfits and posed in front of the mirror before showing Masachika, who praised her by using every compliment he had ever learned from comics, video games, and anime. His sense of shame slowly dulled while Alisa slowly began to enjoy herself. It was just as Masachika expected. She didn't have any friends to go shopping with, and whenever she went shopping with her sister, Maria would simply say, *"Oh, you look so cute,"* no matter what Alisa wore, so this was the first time she ever had someone compliment her in such detail like this.

What should I choose next? Decisions ♪, decisions. ♪

She was in such a good mood now that she was even humming to herself in her head while she picked out her clothes. If Yuki were there, she would laugh at Alisa for being so easily charmed, but Alisa herself was not self-aware enough to realize this. Instead, she mirthfully reached out for outfits that she usually would not wear "just in case."

This is a little too...risqué, isn't it? I'm sure Kuze will still compliment me, though.

It was a miniskirt and camisole that was far skimpier than anything else she had worn. The miniskirt seemed especially short, since Alisa naturally had such long legs, to the point that describing it as *below the crotch* would be more fitting than *above the knees*. It was something she would normally never wear under any circumstances, and even if she did, she would never wear it in front of a boy. However, Masachika's constant praise helped her drown out the faint voice of reason in the back of her head. In fact, she was so excited that she didn't even realize there were two people on the other side of the curtain now…

"What do you thi—?"

Only after she leaned forward and placed her right index finger on her cheek with a wink did she notice that Yuki was standing right next to Masachika. The moment their eyes met, Alisa's winking eye froze shut. Meanwhile, Yuki was blinking at the sight while holding two paper bags full of anime goods.

"Wooow, Alya. Sexy."

"…Yeah."

Yuki whistled with a natural expression while Masachika averted his gaze with an indescribable look on his face, instantly dragging Alisa back into reality. The blood drained from her face before immediately rushing back into her cheeks.

"…Right."

Alisa pulled her crimson, twitching cheeks into a tight smile while swiftly shutting the curtain and quietly curling up into a ball.

"<I want to disappear…,>" she muttered in a fading voice after looking at herself in the mirror once more.

"What'd Alya say?"

"She said she wanted to disappear."

"Heh! What an innocent little babyyy. Ha-ha!"

"You're sick."

Even a whisper that soft couldn't escape these two siblings.

After calming down and purchasing two of the outfits she had tried on, Alisa left the shopping center with Masachika and Yuki, and they started heading home. Alisa's mood, however, did not get any better even after they got on the train, and Masachika and Yuki simply played on their phones without chatting as if they were trying not to make the situation any worse for her.

"Well, see you Monday, Alya."

"I had a lot of fun today. Let's do this again sometime."

"Yeah, see you two Monday."

The train pulled up to Masachika and Yuki's stop. After they got off the train, Alisa immediately sank into her seat.

"<That didn't just happen…>"

Alisa thought back to how she'd made a fool of herself (by her standards) earlier, making her want to fall to the floor and writhe.

"<I bet they think I'm some sort of promiscuous schoolgirl after seeing me in that short skirt…>"

She buried herself in the paper bag resting in her lap while the shame and regret consumed her…when she suddenly realized something weird.

"…Hmm?"

It was very weird. Why did they get off at the same station? Their houses were three stations apart, so it wouldn't make sense for them to get off at the same station.

"What the…?"

There were only a few possible explanations. They were still not planning on going home yet. Or maybe they were planning on going home together?

"What in the…?"

And her assumption was technically correct. There was no way Yuki could bring her anime merchandise back home to the Suou household, so she decided to enjoy her spoils of war at the Kuze residence—circumstances that Alisa was completely unaware of.

"Are those two really…?"

But she managed to stop the seed of doubt from growing any more than that.

Wait. No. They probably just wanted to stop by another shop before heading home.

After persuading herself that it was all in her head, Alisa suddenly remembered something else and pulled out her phone.

Hold on. What did she call it again? A "boyfriend shirt"?

While relying on her memories, Alisa searched the internet until she found a certain image, causing her eyes to open wide.

"Huh?!"

The random squeal caught the surrounding passengers' attention, but Alisa was too deep in thought to care. It was a picture from a comic geared toward young women. A boy and girl were facing each other while sitting on the bed, but while the girl was wearing a baggy collared shirt and faintly smiling, the boy...was completely bare from the waist up.

W-w-w-w-wait, wait, wait! What did she mean by that?!

The seed of doubt she was suppressing shot powerfully into the air and pierced the ceiling.

Wait! What?! Are they...?!

Alisa gazed in wonder at the erotic scene as she replaced the characters with Masachika and Yuki in her head before erasing the thought in a panic.

What is going on?!

She spent the rest of her time on the train agonizing about what it all meant without ever finding an answer.

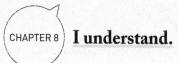

CHAPTER 8 **I understand.**

"Sigh... Is it just me, or is she starting to become more demanding?" muttered Masachika to himself after school while he read the message Yuki had sent him. The student council apparently needed to go buy some supplies, but she wouldn't be able to do it because she had something urgent to take care of. Therefore, she asked Masachika to go in her place.

> Pretty please? You're my favorite brother in the whole wide world ♡♡♡

"..."
He was annoyed by how obvious she was being while trying to flatter him, but he felt too mentally drained to fight.
"Yeah, I'll go. I'll go, but...," mumbled Masachika as he simply replied, Okay.

> Hooray! You're the best! I love you sooo much ♡

"Yeah, yeah."
Masachika smirked at the barrage of heart emoji she thereupon sent him, then stuffed his phone into his pocket and headed to the student council room. When all was said and done, he was very soft-hearted when it came to his sister and couldn't say no to her. Some people in society might even say he had a sister complex.
"Anyone here?"

After knocking on the door, Masachika stepped inside to find two people already waiting there.

"Oh, hey. Thanks for coming to help us again."

"Don't thank me. I'm just trying to fill in for Yuki, since she asked me to."

One of the two people was Touya Kenzaki, and the other was…

"Oh my. So you're Kuze? I'm Maria Mikhailovna Kujou, Alya's older sister and the secretary of the student council. Nice to meet you," Maria cheerfully greeted as she smiled gently.

"Hey. Nice to finally get to meet you, too."

She was the polar opposite of her sister, thought Masachika while he gave her a small bow.

"I was told I'd be going out to buy some supplies with you, but…?"

"Call me Masha. A friend of Alya's is a friend of mine, after all."

"Oh… Okay…"

As Maria gleefully approached him, Masachika recoiled slightly. *Sh-she's so outgoing and nice*, he thought.

"You could even call me Ms. Masha if you want."

"Oh… I think I'll just call you Masha."

Masachika bashfully averted his gaze until Maria stopped right in front of him, cupped his right hand with her hands, and gently shook his hand.

"Sounds good to me…"

Her smile and handshake could bewitch any man in the world, but when she looked at Masachika and saw him close-up, her cheerful expression instantly disappeared. She opened her usually heavy-lidded, almond-shaped eyes wide as she assumed a completely serious expression.

"I-is everything okay?"

Masachika instinctively stepped back when he noticed her sudden transformation, but he couldn't take another step away because she was tightly holding his right hand.

"Kuze… What's your first name?"

"Huh? Masachika…"

"Masa…chika…"

Her expression was so serious that it was almost frightening. Maria was staring at him so hard that it was as if she could burn a hole through his face. A beautiful, older woman who he had essentially just met was holding his hand while staring into his eyes. Masachika's heart was racing with excitement, but that excitement soon turned into anxiety.

"What's wrong, Maria? You see a ghost possessing him or something?"

"Wouldn't be the first time someone has ghosted me."

"Ha-ha. Good one."

Touya gave Masachika the thumbs-up after his quick, smooth pun, and the sudden joke caused Maria to slowly blink a few times before her usual sweet smile curled her lips once more.

"Oh, sorry. I was just thinking, 'So this is Alya's friend I keep hearing about,' and I started daydreaming a little."

After letting go of Masachika, Maria placed a hand on her cheek while apologetically tilting her head to the side. Then, as if to pull herself together, she clapped her hands together and said:

"<Ready to go?>"

Masachika blinked at the sudden Russian. Of course, he understood what she'd said, but he had been pretending to not understand Russian in front of Maria's little sister, Alisa, so he had no choice but to play dumb.

"I'm sorry. What was that?" he asked, feigning a look of innocence. Maria's eyes opened wide for a brief second, but her smile almost immediately returned.

"My apologies. I was just asking if you were ready to go."

"Oh, sure. Let's go."

"Anyway, President, we'll be back soon."

"Thanks a lot, Maria."

"My pleasure."

"I'm counting on you, too."

"I won't let you down."

They briefly bowed to Touya and left the room.

"By the way, Yuki said we needed to go buy some supplies, but she didn't exactly tell me what."

"Mainly stuff we need to use in the student council room."

"Oh... It sounds like the situation's a little different in high school. We used to just order everything from the manufacturers back in middle school."

"We still do that for the basic necessities, but these are things we're going to be using every day, so ideally, we would actually enjoy them. Take tea, for instance. You would probably want to smell it before actually buying it."

"Oh, that makes sense...which makes it even stranger that someone like me is helping, since I'm not even in the student council."

"Then why not join the student council? Problem solved."

"I'm not interested."

"Really? That's too bad."

Maria shrugged as if she really was disappointed, causing Masachika to smirk.

"I'm good at holding bags, though, so don't be shy."

"I'm counting on you."

Being an outsider, it would probably be better to keep quiet and just carry whatever Maria picked out instead, thought Masachika, but it wasn't that simple.

"This incense smells sooo good. Let's try them all out and see—"

"I don't think using incense in the student council room is a good idea. You should probably stick to just using it at home."

"Oh my gosh! Look at this cat plushie. It looks just like Alya! Oh, I know! How about we get a plushie that resembles each member of the student council and then decorate the room with them?"

"It'd look like a gift shop! There's no way the president's going to feel comfortable in a room like that!"

"This lion wearing glasses right here looks *just* like him."

"Were you even listening to me? I said— What the...?! That *does* look just like him!"

"Looks like we're going with the lion, then."

"Wait! Yes, it looks like him, but you can't decorate the student council room with stuffed animals!"

"What?! Come on! ♪"

"No, you 'come on'!"

"Mmm... Fine. But I'm still going to buy the cat plushie for myself, since it's so cute."

"You can't buy it together with the rest of this! The receipts have to be separate! Alya's the accountant. Remember? She'd be pissed!"

Masachika knew it was going to be bad the moment they stepped into a variety store, but it was even worse than he thought it would be. She was far more free-spirited and spontaneous than he could have ever imagined. Maria was darting her eyes all around the shop while selecting things inappropriate for the student council room, and she wasn't joking around. Masachika was too busy correcting her and guiding her in the right direction to even worry about his original plan of keeping quiet and carrying whatever they bought.

It's hopeless. Is she always this way? Because I don't see how Alya deals with this every day.

They somehow managed to only purchase the bare necessities, but by the time they started heading to their final destination, the tea shop, Masachika was already exhausted. He fulfilled his role of holding the bags and glanced down at Maria, who was holding on to the cat plushie as she walked. Even a grade schooler would have a difficult time getting away with walking around town while holding a stuffed animal, but it didn't seem that strange when Maria did it, for some reason.

I'm sure most people passing by are probably thinking, I wish I were that cat, *so I guess that's part of the reason why.*

Masachika thought that as he gazed at the two melons crushing the plushie's head from behind…when he suddenly imagined Alisa glaring at him as if he were garbage, and he flinched.

Come on. Give me a break. What kind of guy wouldn't stare at ones as incredible as these? We can't help it. That's the sad nature of man.

He apologized to Alisa in his head.

"Kuze, we're here."

"Oh! Sorry!"

"…? Is everything okay?"

"No— I mean—yes! It's nothing."

Although Maria curiously tilted her head, she didn't pry and instead promptly walked inside the tea shop.

"Hey, Masha? Maybe I should hold that for you."

"Oh, thanks. I'm counting on you to take good care of Mewlisa for me, okay?"

"M-Mewlisa…"

His cheek twitched at the incredible name given to the plushie while he gently took it out of her arms.

Great… Now I look like a creep!

People might nervously laugh if they saw a high school girl holding a stuffed animal, but a high school boy? They would intentionally try to avoid eye contact while keeping a straight face. And yet…

"Oh my! You look so cute!"

"You need to get your eyes checked."

Maria mirthfully smiled as if something had tugged at her heartstrings, and she swiftly pulled out her smartphone to take a picture.

"Say cheese."

"I'm not letting you take a picture."

"Oh, come on. Please?"

Masachika held one of their shopping bags in front of the camera's lens. He was no longer hesitating to treat her as an equal and tell her exactly what was on his mind.

"Didn't we come here to look at tea?"

"Oh yeah! …Hey, it's the owner! Long time no see!"

After managing to avoid having his picture taken, Masachika

waited in the corner of the room as he watched her. Maria seemed to be a regular here. She talked with the elderly owner while smelling various types of tea.

"What do you think I should get?"

"I don't really know anything about tea. Plus, it's not like I'm going to be drinking any."

Maria asked for feedback, perhaps worried that he was bored, but Masachika politely declined.

I'm sure Yuki would have been able to help, though.

A young gentlewoman of the Suou household would surely be knowledgeable about tea brands. While thinking that, a female clerk suddenly came walking out from the back of the shop with paper cups of tea on a tray. It appeared it was time to taste the tea that Maria was curious about.

"Mm-hmm! This is delicious. Kuze, you have to try this."

She affectionately smiled with a paper cup touching her lips while waving Masachika over. There was only one thing that came to his mind, though.

A-am I about to have an indirect kissing scene?!

These were the types of events in games where an oblivious girl casually handed the protagonist a water bottle or cup she was drinking from, but most rom-com protagonists' embarrassment would be rewarded with this fleeting moment of happiness!

I'm not like them, though.

Acting embarrassed meant defeat. Thinking too hard about it meant defeat. Masachika was well aware of that. He had to be cool about it. He had to look like a badass!

"All right…"

After placing the bags on the floor, he suavely walked (in his mind) over to Maria, and—

"And here's a cup for you, sir."

"Thanks."

—the female clerk handed him his own cup, which he accepted

with a smile. They'd apparently prepared enough tea for both of them. What a thoughtful, generous tea shop...but unfortunately, Masachika wasn't exactly thrilled.

Gaaaaaaaaah! How embarrassing! I'm such a loser! Ahhh!

While he may have been wearing a smile while taking a sip of his tea, he was internally screaming in agony.

"It tastes good, doesn't it?"

"Yeah, this is seriously good."

"Right?"

"Yep."

He may have been acting like nothing was wrong, but he was still inwardly writhing with despair. It was a prime example of a nerd who couldn't tell 2D and real life apart. A sad reality for some.

"Oh, you're back. I really appreciate— Whoa. That's a lot of stuff."

Touya, who was doing paperwork in the student council room, saw Maria holding a stuffed animal and smirked.

"Isn't it adorable?"

"Yeah, it's cute, but you're not going to decorate the room with it, right?"

"Can I?"

"Please don't."

"Hey, where should I put all this stuff?" asked Masachika, holding the shopping bags into the air. Touya stood from his chair and took a look inside them.

"So let's see what you bought... Yep, plain ol' supplies. Good work, Kuze. I don't even want to imagine what would've happened if I let Maria go shopping all by herself..."

"The student council room would have looked like some sort of theme-park gift shop.

"...Thank you. I really appreciate what you did."

Touya solemnly patted Masachika on the shoulder after seeing Maria hugging the cat plushie, as if he had a good idea what would have happened.

"So? What do you say, Kuze? Change your mind about joining the student council?"

"No, but...I don't mind helping every once in a while."

"Then why not register at the very least? It could be in name only. We're not going to force you, but what do you have to lose?"

"Oh, you agree, Maria?"

"I couldn't become a member in name only. By the way, I get why Yuki wants me to join, but what would the president want with me?" Masachika asked skeptically, but Touya simply rubbed his chin as if he was the confused one.

"Hmm... I'm actually curious as to why you don't want to join. I find it hard to believe the taxing work is the only thing keeping you from it."

"...Because I don't deserve to be a member."

Masachika had neither a strong desire for the position nor the drive to take on the responsibility that came along with it, so he believed he didn't deserve it. A shadow clouded Masachika's forced smile, but Touya simply raised a curious eyebrow and tilted his head.

"I don't think that at all. If anything, you proved you could do it when you were the vice president in middle school."

"I know I'm not right for the job because of my experience. Besides, the only reason I became vice president in the first place was because Yuki asked me to... It wasn't like I took on the responsibility because there was something I wanted to do."

"And? What's wrong with that?"

"Huh?"

Masachika lifted his head, taken aback by the tone of Touya's voice. Touya then grinned, puffed out his chest, and continued:

"I only became the president of the student council because I wanted a girl to like me. If you think *you* joined for all the wrong reasons, then I've got you beat! Ha-ha-ha!"

"W-wait. Seriously?"

He was caught off guard by how Touya could say something like that with such confidence, and his eyes opened wide. Touya tapped his smartphone a couple of times, then showed him a picture he had saved.

"Check it out."

"…? Uh… Is this your little brother?"

"That's me during my third year of middle school."

"What?!"

The boy in the picture could not look any more different from Touya. To be blunt, he was a very plump, nerdy-looking kid. His hair was a mess, his glasses were far from stylish, and his face was covered in acne. It didn't help that he was as tall as he was wide and was sheepishly hunching over. There was the slightest trace of this boy in the Touya whom Masachika knew.

"As you can see, I was your stereotypical loser two years ago. My grades weren't good, and I wasn't athletic, either. To be honest, I didn't even like school itself that much, but I ended up falling in love with a girl way out of my league: one of the two beauties of Seiren Academy."

"Wait. Do you mean…?"

"Yep, the vice president, Chisaki Sarashina."

Basically, everyone at school knew that the president and vice president were dating. Even Masachika, who had absolutely no interest in gossip, had a rough idea. But he always thought it was simply two elite students at the top of the school caste dating. Never did he imagine that an underdog at the bottom of the school caste managed to pull off an upset win.

"After that, I worked my ass off to become someone good enough for her. Becoming president was nothing more than the first step to achieve that goal. I did it all for myself. Still think your motive was impure?"

"Ha-ha-ha… I see what you mean."

Masachika could only laugh at how proudly Touya admitted that. He had no idea what to say.

"So who cares what your reason for joining is? Even Maria here only joined because Chisaki asked her to."

"Really?"

"Yep. I had been interested in it before, though," admitted Maria with an attractive smile. Her expression became slightly more serious as she gently added:

"I don't think that motives matter as long as you produce results. Whether you join for love or friendship is up to you. All you need to do is work hard for your fellow students."

"Really...?"

"Of course. If it were any other way, that'd mean that politicians had to be saints to run for their positions, and, well..."

"Ha-ha-ha. You've got a point." Masachika laughed awkwardly.

"She's right. It doesn't matter why you joined. You and Yuki achieved outstanding results, and there's absolutely no reason why you should feel embarrassed or guilty about that," chimed in Touya. Those words strongly resonated with Masachika. He had always felt guilty deep down inside. No matter what he achieved, he always felt there was someone better for the job, and that thought haunted him. The guilt of stealing that position from someone had cast a shadow over his heart. People could praise someone for every little thing they did, but it would be meaningless if they never acknowledged it themselves. Glory would feel empty without self-respect. But Masachika was finally able to give his past self some credit thanks to Touya and Maria.

"Maybe you only want to join the student council to help someone else become president? Do it. Chisaki, Maria, and I welcome you with open arms, and I'm not going to let anyone stop you," vowed Touya as he proudly, fearlessly smirked, and Masachika almost wanted to cry. Was it the happiness of feeling like he had been forgiven for his past? Or was he simply being drawn toward Touya's radiant glow?

"...I'll think about it."

"Great. Take your time. Think about it long and hard. That's a privilege of being young."

"You're still young, too, President. ♪ You honestly don't look like you're still in high school, though."

"Ha-ha-ha! I get that a lot! Someone even mistook me for a college student the other day!"

Masachika couldn't help but crack a small smile as he watched his kindhearted schoolmates laugh cheerfully.

Joining in order to help someone become the next president…

He ruminated on Touya's words until someone naturally came to mind. He was surprised, though, because that person wasn't Yuki…

"By the way, where's Alya?" asked Masachika, looking around the room. Although it was a rather sudden change of topic, Touya didn't seem to be bothered as he replied:

"Oh, she's acting as an arbitrator for a bit of trouble between two of the sports clubs… She's taking a lot longer than I thought she would, though."

"'Trouble'? Do you mean…?"

"Don't worry. There wasn't a fight. A physical one, at least."

Apparently, the soccer club and the baseball club were having an argument about who had the right to use the schoolyard, since they both went there for practice. Around this time every year, the baseball club would be practicing in the schoolyard frequently for their upcoming games. However, the soccer club spoke out this year. They had matches to prepare for as well, so they asked the baseball club to hand over their schoolyard rights.

"The baseball club argued that this was how things have been every year, while the soccer club argued that it didn't make sense for them to get special treatment, since their performance hasn't been particularly strong. The soccer club has, in fact, been very successful this past year. Meanwhile, the baseball team has been losing members and shrinking these past few years. So I can see where they're coming from. It's going to be hard to find common ground."

"So Alya went to see if she could help them work things out?"

"Yeah. Usually, when there's trouble between two clubs, Chisaki's the one who handles things, but she had something important to take care of at the kendo club today, so she couldn't make it. I figured this would be good experience for Alisa, but it looks like she's having a hard time."

Touya looked at the clock, then outside the window at the clubhouse.

"Should we be worried?"

"Hmm? Well, I'm sure things will get pretty heated, but it's not going to turn into an all-out brawl or anything." Touya shrugged. Maria was showing no signs of worrying, either, as she organized the supplies they had just bought. However, Masachika couldn't help but think back to when Alisa got into an argument with that intoxicated businessman, making him feel uneasy.

"Anyway, I should get going."

"All right. Take care."

"Thanks a lot for helping me shop today. I promise I'll make it up to you."

"I'm looking forward to it."

Although distracted, Masachika said his good-byes and left the student council room.

"I should go make sure it hasn't gotten physical," he muttered to himself before setting out not for the school entrance, but for the clubhouse.

"Yeah, bro! I get that you do this every year, but they're just local, friendly matches, right? We're practicing for this year's tournament! It's very important!"

"These matches are important to us because they're friendly! We're building relationships with other schools. You guys are being unreasonable!"

The soccer team's clubroom was on the verge of exploding as they argued with around a dozen older students from the baseball team.

Neither group was planning on backing down as they glared daggers at each other.

"Let's all calm down. Criticizing each other isn't going to get us anywhere."

Alisa tried to mediate for the umpteenth time, but it didn't seem to be working. She had prepared a new practice spot, a riverbed near school, to use in the negotiation, but now they were arguing about who would use the schoolyard and who would use the riverbed. They were talking in circles at this point, and now half the conversation was essentially them hurling insults at each other. Alisa tried her best to find a point of compromise, but the two groups were far too heated up to even listen.

"Listen, the soccer team has way more members! It would be easier for you guys to take the riverbed!"

"You get a bigger budget because of that, though! And now you're trying to bully us so you can steal the only thing we have left? The place where we practice?"

"Okay, okay! Relax!"

Alisa was trying to calm them down, but she was getting close to her breaking point. No matter how tough she was, being surrounded by a bunch of older, athletic guys was terrifying. It didn't help that they were ignoring her proposals and insulting each other. And if they started hurling those insults at her? Even Alisa would mentally break. She managed to hold it together because of her strong sense of responsibility and stubbornness, but even then, she was reaching her limit.

Nobody's listening to me. I guess I really can't...

She couldn't reach them emotionally. Alisa always had a faint feeling that she didn't have what it took. She'd always look down on others, thinking they wouldn't be able to keep up with her, and she refused to try to understand or compromise with them.

And these were the consequences. Who would listen to someone like that? How would someone who only arrogantly forced their reasoning on others without considering how they felt ever be able to connect with others?

I'm all alone...

That fact chilled her heart like poison.

It wasn't anything she wasn't prepared for, though. Alisa was the one who chose this way of life. It was because she only viewed others as rivals and lived her life as if it was a competition that she couldn't lose. These were the consequences of her decisions.

I know that... I know that, but...!

But...!

"<Help...>"

But no one here would be able to understand her feeble cry in Russian. She couldn't throw away her pride and run away. She couldn't cry. She couldn't even ask for help. *That's why you're always going to be alone*, she thought. And while she truly believed that, she strained her trembling voice and said:

"<Somebody...please help me...>"

That weak, pathetic murmur was an SOS—a desperate cry for help that took everything she had to make. They were the words of a lonely girl who knew they would simply be drowned out by the angry insults being hurled around the room...or so she thought.

Rattle!

Everyone looked over as the door suddenly slid open. Standing at the entrance was your ordinary male student. The color of his tie made it clear he was a first-year, and he had an average build, making him the skinniest guy there. Yet everyone caught their breath the instant he glared at them. They were swallowed by his aura. Even the older students from the soccer club fell silent before his gaze. The male student boldly stepped into the room...then gently smiled and said:

"Hey, the student council sent me to help. I'm Masachika Kuze. I'm in charge of general affairs."

◇

After arriving in front of the soccer team's clubroom, Masachika overheard Alisa's solitary struggle from outside.

Alya, you're not going to solve this today.

Masachika came to this decision while hearing Alisa run out of things to say. Both groups were too worked up. They needed to make a fresh start and talk at a later date after cooling off. Someone as smart as Alisa surely understood this, but she seemed to be so anxious to solve the task she was given that she didn't know when to call it quits.

I feel bad, but I guess this will be a good learning experience for her.

They were not going to reach an agreement at this rate. If anything, it was going to end without a resolution, but they could discuss things again at a later date after cooling off. At any rate, nobody wanted to hear what an outsider would have to say. Plus, saying anything would also hurt Alisa's pride.

"You can do it, Alya."

After that brief whisper, Masachika turned on his heel when…

"<Help…>"

…he heard Alisa's faint SOS signal and froze. It was a feeble, desperate voice. It was something he had never heard before: Alisa asking for help. Masachika's chest tightened, and he pulled at his hair.

Dammit! Why did you have to say that?!

He should've left a few moments ago. Then he wouldn't have had to hear her say that. What kind of sad excuse of an SOS was that? She should have just asked the president or her sister for help if she really wanted it. But she couldn't. That's why she was always alone. That was why…

"<Somebody…please help me… Nobody understands that I…>"

This is why I can't just abandon her. He softly muttered:

"^{I understand}
"Японял."

Masachika understood that she needed help. He understood everything, so he combed his hair back before turning toward the door.

While most students were bewildered by this intruder's sudden appearance, a few of them, including the club leader of the baseball team, uttered his name in surprise.

"Kuze…"

They were the ones who knew him from middle school when he had been in the student council.

"Kuze…"

Alisa called his name. Her voice was brimming with astonishment and wonder but was also imploring. After patting her on the back, Masachika stood in front of her as if to protect her.

"The president gave me a brief rundown of what was going on. You're arguing about who's going to practice in the schoolyard and who's going to use the riverbed. Is that the gist of it?"

"That about sums it up."

"Great."

It was the captain of the baseball team, having remained silent this entire time for some reason as the others had hurled insults, who answered Masachika's question. He turned a gaze, half-hopeful and half-trusting, toward Masachika, who then looked at each individual student.

"Then how about this? Considering how many members are in each club, the baseball team should move to the riverside for practice. In return, the soccer team should send some members to help them move," he suggested. The soccer captain was bewildered while the baseball captain became irate.

"What?! Why do we have to get the short end of the stick?"

"Why do we have to be the ones who practice at the riverside?!"

It was only natural that they argued, but all their complaints came to a sudden end when a certain member of the soccer club spoke up.

"If the baseball club is okay with that, then we managers would be more than willing to help."

It was one of the female captains in the soccer club who spoke up.

She was the chief manager and extremely popular among the male club members due to her cute appearance and dedication to the athletes.

"If she'd help, then…"

Members in the baseball club began to warm up to the idea after her unexpected proposal, but now the soccer club began to show reluctance.

"If they're going to let us use the schoolyard, then this is the least we can do in return."

Her words alone were enough to shut them up.

"We're fine with those conditions. How about you?" asked the leader of the baseball club, since he could tell his club was okay with it. The leader of the soccer club subtly frowned but nodded in response.

"It's settled, then. Just stop by the student council tomorrow to apply for permission," instructed Masachika, wrapping up the meeting after the problem surprisingly resolved itself.

Masachika and Alisa were making their way down the hall in the club-house en route to the main building. They quietly walked without exchanging a word or even glancing in each other's direction.

"Hey… Sorry about that," eventually said Masachika as if he couldn't bear the silence any longer, but Alisa shot him a quizzical glance. "I guess I kind of stole your thunder by barging in and doing all that."

"…It's fine," Alisa replied dryly before facing forward once more. Then, still gazing straight ahead, she said, "Hey. Why did you make a proposal like that?"

"Hmm?"

"Under normal circumstances, the baseball club would have immediately shot down an idea like that. But it looked like you almost knew that the manager would offer to help."

"Wow… I'm impressed you noticed."

"Of course I did. You were staring at her the entire time the base-ball club was protesting."

She really is observant, he thought.

"What I'm about to tell you is just between you and me, okay?" exclaimed Masachika as if he was going to disclose a secret.

"...? Sure."

"That manager...is actually going out with the leader of the base-ball club."

"What?!"

Shocked, Alisa turned to look at Masachika.

"You remember how the leader of the baseball club didn't say a word the entire time they were arguing? It's because he didn't want to say anything harsh, since his girlfriend was in the other group. They say you can't mix business with personal affairs, and now we see why. That's life, though."

"I had no idea..."

"Plus, she knew they were asking for way too much, so it must have been really awkward for her. That's why I knew she'd jump in and offer to help."

"...Oh."

"The guys in the baseball club are happy that some cute girls are going to help them practice, and the soccer club is happy since they get the schoolyard all to themselves. And those two lovebirds are happy because they get to spend time together during practice, despite being members of different clubs. What a perfect ending to all this!" claimed Masachika.

"I feel like the guys in the baseball club who have no idea what just happened kind of got the short end of the stick, though," he added with a laugh, causing Alisa to crack a slight smile as well.

"...!"

But Masachika's smirk twitched slightly when he saw a male student standing at the end of the hallway connected to the main building.

"Were you able to work something out?"

"President…"

It was Touya, smiling and unfazed by the fact that Masachika and Alisa were together, as if he had known this was going to happen.

"The baseball club agreed to give up the schoolyard and use the riverbed in return for the soccer club's managers helping them with practice… Kuze was the one who worked things out with them," explained Alisa in a detached tone.

"Really? Good work, Alisa."

But Touya didn't say any more than that. Masachika, however, glared at him with a scornful, rebellious gaze.

"This was all part of your plan, huh?"

"Hmm? Not exactly."

"The fact that you didn't deny it and say 'What are you talking about?' shows that you were at least somewhat expecting this to happen, though."

"Heh… You got me."

Touya raised his hands in surrender, killing Masachika's enthusiasm and causing him to sigh.

"So? Have you made a decision?"

"…"

He knew all along that this would happen, thought Masachika as he raised a white flag.

"Well… Although I'm unworthy of the honor, I suppose I wouldn't mind taking a seat at the student council."

"I'm glad to have you." Touya smiled while Masachika grinned bitterly, knowing he was no match for the president's cunning. Alisa stood back and watched with a complicated look on her face as they firmly shook hands with their contrasting smiles.

EPILOGUE) **Take My Hand**

"Sigh… I'm not a fan of getting played like that, but I guess it was going to happen sometime."

After Touya had told Masachika to stop by the next day with the paperwork and told Alisa that she was done for the day, Masachika and Alisa walked toward the school gate under the dark night sky. While Masachika was grumbling to himself, Alisa followed closely behind in silence with a slightly downcast expression. But when they were about halfway to the school entrance, Alisa suddenly stopped.

"Hey."

"Hmm? What's up?"

"…"

Masachika looked back at Alisa, but she didn't say a thing. Her blue eyes held mixed emotions while she stared hard into his eyes, and he quietly stared back into hers.

"Are you really going to join the student council?"

"Yeah."

"Is that…?"

She paused for a moment before firmly continuing:

"Is that so you can run as vice president alongside Yuki?"

"…What if it was?"

He replied to Alisa's question with a question.

"Would you give up and drop out of the race if that was the case?"

After briefly closing her eyes as if to smother any dependence she was feeling, Alisa opened her eyes once more, revealing a shimmering glow.

"…No," she replied to his provocation. "I am going to become the student council president, no matter what…even if that means I'll be running against you. I'm not going to give up."

Masachika snorted out a laugh and broke into a smile. That powerful light in her eyes was what he wanted to see—what he wanted to protect. He was attracted to that brilliant glow of her noble soul, and until this point, he had helped her from the shadows to prevent that glow from ever clouding over. But not anymore. From now on…

"…Okay," Masachika said, nodding with his eyes closed.

"…!"

Alisa pressed her lips together tightly and faintly lowered her gaze until Masachika suddenly opened his eyes wide and declared:

"Then I'm going to make you the president."

"Huh…?"

Her expression wavered in bewilderment, but Masachika looked her right in the eyes and held out his hand to her.

"I will do everything in my power to make you president if that's what you wish. You won't be alone anymore. From now on, I will be by your side to support you. So don't say a word and just take my hand! Alya!"

Countless questions popped into her head before being replaced by another: *Why? Why me? Why not Yuki?* But each question melted away before his decisive gaze without ever reaching her lips.

Oh… That's why…

Alisa suddenly realized what was going on. Masachika saw right through her and knew how stubborn she was. That was why he told her not to say another word and take his hand. She didn't need to ask him for help this way.

Yeah…

Alisa was always alone. She only saw others as competition and looked down on them. She never thought there would be someone she could trust to be there for her. But if there was someone who would accept every part of her, no matter how hopeless she might be... If there was someone there for her unconditionally...then...

"...!"

Not even Alisa could identify the emotions welling up in her heart. Was she touched? Wishful? Delighted? It was all those things and yet none of them. She was swallowed by the furious waves of emotions, almost to the point of tears, but she didn't cry. She didn't want the boy in front of her to see her that way because he probably didn't want to see her like that, either. Alisa threw back her shoulders and proudly faced forward. *I wasn't looking for help*, she thought. She would neither try to suck up to nor cling on to him. She took his hand as an equal.

"Good. I'm looking forward to working with you, Alya," said Masachika with a smirk, as an equal partner, and his unobtrusive kindness brought a smile to Alisa's face like a flower in full bloom.

"Thank you."

The voice of her heart slipped out between her slightly parted lips. And then...

...the words of gratitude that accidentally slipped off Alisa's tongue and the smile from the bottom of her heart—a smile Masachika had never seen before...

...made his heart race.

And at the same time, it reminded him of a warm memory from long ago: *that girl's* smile.

Wh-what is this feeling?

His heart hammered against his chest like a drum. It was the beat of love—something he never expected to feel again after *that girl* had disappeared.

Ha-ha... Seriously? I didn't know I still had emotions like this.

He couldn't take his eyes off the girl in front of him. Her hands were so warm. The heat— The pain...?

"Ow, ow, ow! What the...?!"

Before he realized it, Alisa's smile had turned into something plastered on her face, and she was tightly squeezing his hand like a

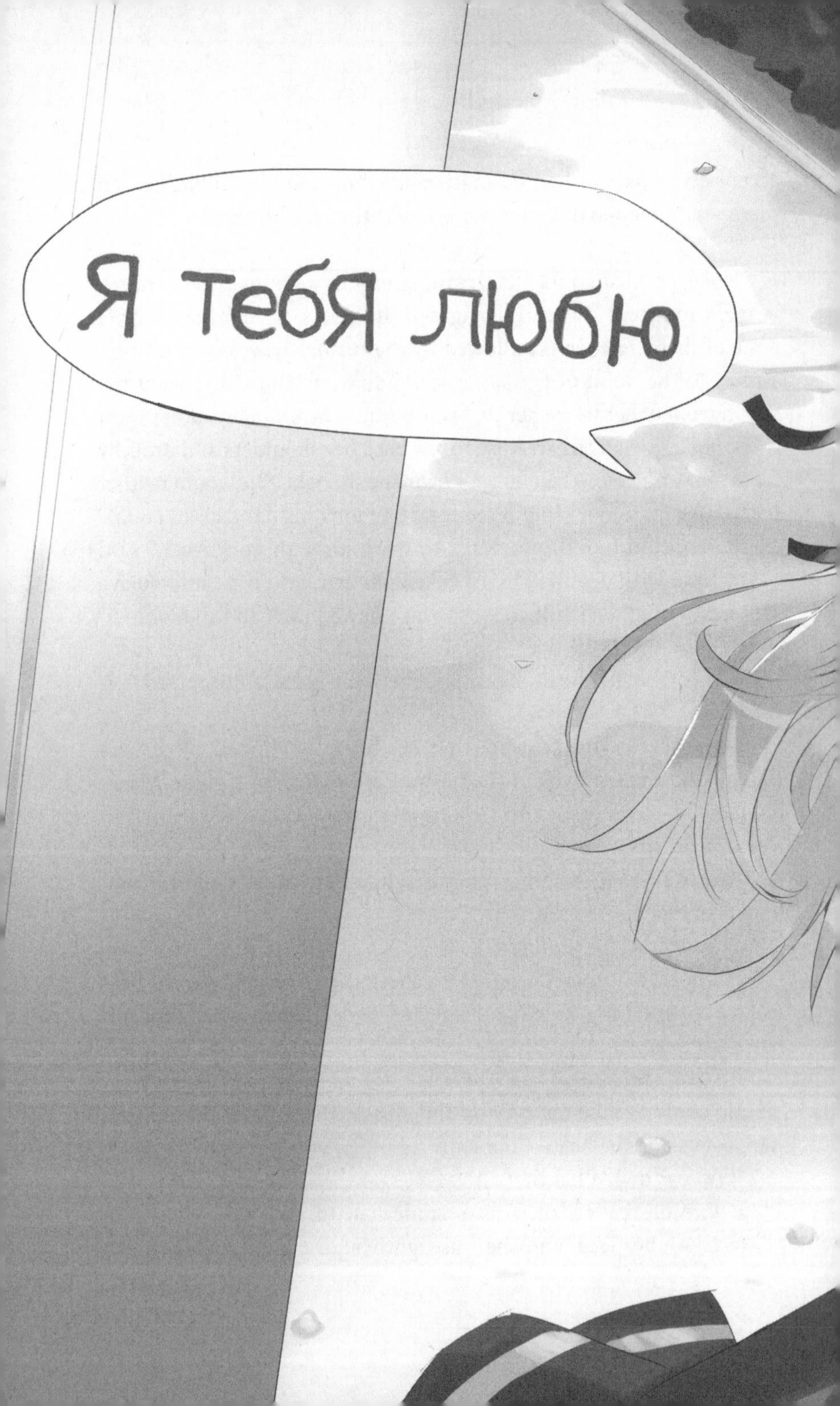
Я тебя люблю

vise. He shrieked while curling his body with a pleading, quizzical gaze, but his eyes were met with a subzero glare.

"Were you thinking about another woman just now?" she asked quietly.

"How'd you know?! Oops…"

He immediately regretted his knee-jerk response, but it was already too late. A cold sweat ran down his spine as he realized just how terrible his response was.

Crap, crap, crap! Daydreaming about another girl from your past while the heroine is confessing her love for you is one of the top ten things a rom-com protagonist shouldn't do! I think it was number two when I checked the polls!

Incidentally, the number one thing you shouldn't do was ignore her. Not only would that ruin things with the heroine, but it would also lower the reader's opinion of you, so it was something that should be avoided at all costs.

Is this really the time to be thinking about rom-coms?!

Masachika shut the door to the nerd room in his mind that he had been using to escape reality. However, he had zero experience with love in real life past elementary school, so he had absolutely no clue how he was going to get himself out of this situation. And unfortunately, Alisa spoke up with a chilling smirk before he could figure something out.

"Hey."

"Y-yes?"

"Didn't you just say you were going to be by my side and support me from now on?"

"Huh? Oh yeah. I did say that. Yep."

It was a little embarrassing hearing her repeat what he said, but Masachika wasn't smiling bashfully under her cold, piercing gaze. His face was just twitching.

"And yet you immediately start thinking about Yuki."

"I wasn't thinking about Yuki."

"…Hmph."

"Hey?! Ouch! That seriously hurts!"

The instant he admitted it wasn't Yuki, Alisa squeezed his right hand like a vise again, causing him to scream *Whyyyy?!* to himself.

"Kuze."

"Eep?!"

"If you want me to forgive you, then don't say another word and take what's coming to you."

"...Okay."

After noticing Alisa slowly raising her left hand, Masachika closed his eyes, knowing what was coming. Immediately, a powerful shock hit his cheek like a bolt of lightning, sending him flying back, literally.

"Heh... Heh-heh... Nice slap."

"...You're an idiot."

He gave her the thumbs-up, despite being pathetically curled up on the ground. Although she rolled her eyes, she forgave him just like she promised and extended a hand. After accepting her help up to his feet, Masachika brushed his pants off.

"Ready to go home?"

"Sure."

And just like that, they started their journey home side by side. They were neither snuggling up nor keeping their distance, but they were close enough to naturally hold hands if they tried.

"Whew. I've never been slapped by a girl before. I feel like a real man now."

"Did you hit your head on the ground when you fell?"

"I didn't get a head injury!"

"Yes... Unfortunately, your brain has always rattled inside that head of yours."

"I'll have you know they used to call me the prodigy."

"'The prodigy'? Uh-huh..."

"Wow. You look like you don't believe me."

Relieved they could still banter like they usually did, they were walking slightly closer to each other now, and by the time they reached the entrance to Alisa's apartment complex, her expression included some concern.

"...Is your cheek okay? Do you need some ice?"

"Nah, I'm fine. I can't really feel my right cheek, but it's not so bad if you imagine you just got your wisdom teeth taken out," cheerfully replied Masachika with a slight grimace as if it was unconsciously bothering him.

"That doesn't sound 'fine' at all..."

Alisa shrugged while rolling her eyes when she suddenly looked up as if she had realized something, then held out her index finger and rubbed Masachika's right cheek.

"Do you really have no feeling in your cheek right now?"

"Oh, no... I was joking. I honestly still can't feel much, though," he replied, his heart slightly racing.

"...Uh-huh."

Alisa smirked, then immediately placed a hand on his shoulder as her smile softly drew closer toward him.

"Huh?"

A soft sensation tickled Masachika's right cheek, and he heard a gentle *smack*.

"Huh?"

His eyes opened wide in astonishment while Alisa swiftly leaned away and sent a scornful look his way.

"What are you so shocked about? It was just a little cheek kiss."

"What...? I thought you only touched cheeks when you cheek-kissed..."

"Yes, but you also making a kissing sound when you do it."

"But... Huh?"

That sensation... Was that her cheek or a kiss?!

"Anyway, see you tomorrow."

"O-oh, right... See you tomorrow."

Masachika was there in body but not in spirit when he watched Alisa wave good-bye and walk inside. But after he could no longer see her, he placed a hand on his cheek and crouched.

"Uh...?! S-seriously! Which was it?!"

He rubbed his still-warm cheek, desperately trying to remember the sensation, but no matter how long he thought about it, he couldn't find a definite answer.

"Alyaaa! Can I at least get a hint in Russian?! Please!"

Masachika's pathetic cries echoed down the dark night street.

Afterword

Nice to meet you all. I am the author of this series, Sunsunsun. First, I would like to thank you all for purchasing this novel. If you borrowed this from a friend and made it this far, buy yourself a copy as well. And to the people reading this at the bookstore? Please walk yourself over to the register. Oh, and you? The person who's thinking I'm being a little aggressive in the afterword of my debut novel? Well, I hate to break it to you, but this is how I always drive. You were fooled by the cover jacket. If anything, I'm going as legally fast as I can without the editor getting after me. I'm usually way more of a—

(I apologize for the author's embarrassing behavior. Please give me a moment.)

Anyway, that's the gist of it. Wait. What? I still haven't even written a full page? I was sure I had cleared a thousand words easily. Anyway, I've had my fun, so now it's time to get semiserious. I know I mentioned this on the cover jacket when I introduced myself, but I started out writing web novels on the website Shousetsuka ni Narou. I was never someone who seriously considered having my novel published (like the serious authors). I only did it for fun. I never worked seriously on a serialized series and only stuck to short stories whenever I had an idea. This novel, *Alya Sometimes Hides Her Feelings in Russian,* was originally posted on Shousetsuka ni Narou as a short story until it caught the eye of the editor, and we ended up using the concept to create a brand-new series. It was one of those lucky situations where it started as a one-shot story and leveled up into a serialized series, which you often see happen in weekly manga anthologies. I never dreamed that something like this would happen to me. Since this was going to be a brand-new story, I had to create a new protagonist and heroine as well. What did you think? There's nothing I want more than for you to feel the heroine was cute or the protagonist was cool. Yuki? Yeah, I know she's adorable, so I'm not worried about her (I know).

Anyway, before I go, I wanted to give special thanks to the following people: Natsuki Miyakawa, the editor who has helped me so much in writing this novel; Momoco, who drew the beautiful illustrations; Tapioca, who made the perfect short manga; Sumire Uesaka for doing the voice of the heroine, Alya, and Kouhei Amasaki for doing the voice of Masachika; Shimesaba and Kyousuke Kamishiro for the helpful comments; and everyone who picked up this book. I want to give you all the biggest thanks of the century. Thank you so much! I hope we can meet again in the next volume. Until then.

It's nice to meet you,
Feelings in Russian!

HAVE YOU BEEN TURNED ON TO LIGHT NOVELS YET?

86—EIGHTY-SIX, VOL. 1-11

In truth, there is no such thing as a bloodless war. Beyond the fortified walls protecting the eighty-five Republic Sectors lies the "nonexistent" Eighty-Sixth Sector. The young men and women of this forsaken land are branded the Eighty-Six and, stripped of their humanity, pilot "unmanned" weapons into battle...

Manga adaptation available now!

WOLF & PARCHMENT, VOL. 1-6

The young man Col dreams of one day joining the holy clergy and departs on a journey from the bathhouse, Spice and Wolf. Winfiel Kingdom's prince has invited him to help correct the sins of the Church. But as his travels begin, Col discovers in his luggage a young girl with a wolf's ears and tail named Myuri who stowed away for the ride!

Manga adaptation available now!

SOLO LEVELING, VOL. 1-5

E-rank hunter Jinwoo Sung has no money, no talent, and no prospects to speak of—and apparently, no luck, either! When he enters a hidden double dungeon one fateful day, he's abandoned by his party and left to die at the hands of some of the most horrific monsters he's ever encountered.

Comic adaptation available now!